Broken 2

Billie Dureya Shell

BROKEN 2

Front Cover Image By grafic designer Billie Dureyea Shell & Kenny Writes

First Printing Edition 2020

ISBN 979-1-7350234-5-8

This Book Is Dedicated To

My son my Jr. Little Dureyea
I love you and I always got your back

NO MATTER WHAT.

ACKNOWLEDGEMENT

Once again I want 2 give thank 2 God for this gift I am so grateful for him giving me away 2 provide 4 my family in my house we will alwayz put you first.

To my mother Mclessie Shell you taught me so much and you loved me NO MATTER WHAT I love you so much momma.... What's up on with some bake chicken LOL☺.

To my little sister Glenda I love you and miss you blackie get at ur big brother Lil Sis.

To my Wife Shatoya Shell you get on my damn nerves but I wouldnt trade you 4 anything. In the world I love you more then words can ever express.

To all my children I love y'all Jazmine, Ant'Tuan, Davon, Anthony, David, Lil Dureyea, Alura, Queen Diavion, Cameron, Preniece, Shaniece and Tajh I love u all and I'll 4ever have ur back you all give me a reason 2 smile.......... to my cousin Zane RIP nigga I miss u more then anyone will ever no, your always remembered love you bro.

To my cousin. Ty I miss you thank 4 looking out 4 me and Zane you played a big part in my life and I always looked up to you l love you... Uncle Woody I miss you and love you, you no your my favorite uncle....

To my nigga Jamal love you, my brothers Lawrence and fred thank 4 showing me the game I love yall 4 that.

To my old est sister Nedra love you thank you 4 always having my back. to my family uncles anties cousins etc.. I love y'all even those of you that act funny as fuck

To my dark side nigga's y'all no what it is
YAAH GANG........

Now to all my readers and fans I love you thanks for reading I hope u enjoy this book as much as I enjoy writing them with this Corona Virus 19 shit there ain't shit to do but write so I'm on my shit with that being said y'all be safe cover your face and love each other life is short so love the ones that really love you

I'm gone enjoy the book

AND STAY SAFE

Author

Billie Dureyea Shell

THERE'S NOTHING U CANNOT DO IF U PUT UR MIND 2 IT ....
All you nigga's got EDD money so aint no excuse why you can't get a book LOL

Team Shell

Chapter One

ANIYA

ruce was rushing me as usual. He always did things at the last minute and then wanted me to hurry up and be ready. He act like I did not have kids that I had to make sure were good. He had just told me an hour ago that we was going to head down to Atlanta to meet with his brother Rashad. I didn't understand why he wanted me to meet him when he talked so badly about him. In one breath he would say Rashad is going to help expand our business and in the same breath he would say we were helping Rashad. I was not sure if we were helping him out or he was helping us out. I picked the obvious that his brother was helping us. Hell, we were putting next to nothing in this business and Rashad was paying for everything. All we had to do was show up with a check and negotiate a better deal. I had finally given Bruce some play and I was happy about that. He was the complete opposite of Hakeem. No more beatings and he was attentive to my kids, so that was a plus in my book. To be honest I had fallen in love with Bruce and I knew I was on the right track finally in this relationship. We did everything together except I had not met anyone in his family. I felt like this was a big step although he did not like Rashad, I was happy to be meeting someone. So, the family history went as such. Rashad's mother Renee was the reason that Bruce's father had left his mother. That was all Bruce would talk about because he felt like Renee was a home wrecking hussy. I put two and two together and figured that is why Bruce felt some kind of way about his half brother Rashad. I listened to Bruce rant and rave because had become my lover, friend, and business partner. I thought Hakeem was a mastermind until I met Bruce. Bruce was a partner in my home building company. I wanted to sell it, but he told me all the money I was making why sell just be a partner with him. He invested in the cleaning company also and we made so much money. We wasn't just in Wisconsin anymore we expanded to Chicago. He had a sister Rebecca, who I had not formerly met, run things over there. She was making us a ton of money too. Yes, Bruce had us racking in the money. He was smart when it came to helping me with my businesses that were already established. This was going to be our first start-up company. Bruce and I started out as friends, but the chemistry was there from day one. I loved Bruce he had built my dream home for me and he let me have my freedom. Yes, he was much different than Hakeem. We even did little family outings. Bruce did not have any kids, but he seemed to like my kids. He took Malcolm to softball practice and he played tea party with Deena he was great. Well that was at the beginning of our relationship. To tell the truth things between Bruce and I were kind of changing and I was hoping it was just me and my insecurities that had me feeling this way. Hell, everyone loved Bruce even Cedes he was a great guy, but there was something that I felt like he was hiding. Or maybe I was paranoid because Hakeem was hiding so much from me. Cedes was my personal assistant/nanny and also my kid's siblings mother. That is still crazy to me that I did not know the man that I was living with, had kids by, and loved had three other kids by this woman. What was even crazier was she was his sister's girlfriend. I had learned a lot about Hakeem more in his death than when he was alive. I wished I would have known all of these things before his death. Cedes was running late to get the kids. Chiquita said that she would watch them on such short notice. Cedes was my Nanny but I really did not want to put the kids on her since Vanessa and her had been going through so much lately. Every time I turned around as of lately Cedes was coming in with stories of her and Vanessa fighting. It was over small things but mostly it was because Cedes had started working. Vanessa wanted complete control over Cedes just like her brother. I just wanted Cedes to leave Vanessa before somebody got hurt. Vanessa had been beating on Cedes for I don't know how long and Cedes was fighting back. Good for her but that was just too much for one lone woman to go through. She used to get beat by our baby daddy Hakeem just like I did. She had gotten out with the help of his sister Vanessa. I guess that is why she never wanted to leave because I kept asking her to leave but she was too caught up on the fact that Vanessa had rescued her and taken care of her for so many years. I understood that was one of the reasons why I never left Hakeem well and plus I did not have any money or a support system. Cedes had money though and if she wanted to leave, I would have helped her. I am learning you can't force people to move on from that lifestyle I know that firsthand. All the abuse and bullshit I put up with Hakeem I could not judge anyone. I finished packing my suitcase. I had clothes everywhere over my room. I really did not know how to dress I knew that the Southern weather was different than up North. I tried to put my clothes back in the closet when my phone rung, it was Bruce. "Baby I am waiting on Cedes." I was out of breath. My full figure was slowing me down. I knew I needed to start working out more. "Damn what is you paying her to be late? She is so lazy you need to fire her." He complained. His nasty tone burned my ear. He didn't even know Cedes and he was the one who had just told me about this trip. He was wrong or his statement. I had started to notice that about Bruce he seemed so nice at first, but he was negative person. Everything he had been saying out of his mouth lately was nasty. I don't know if he was just stressed or if this was the real Bruce coming out. I loved the man there was no doubt about it but he had a nasty attitude. "She cool you on the other hand should not have scheduled this trip last minute." I made sure he knew I had an attitude. Hell, who did he think he was? I had been controlled by Hakeem I was not going to jump up for another man. The only reason I did jump up was because this was business and I was always about my business. "I know babe I am sorry, but my bro closed this deal so quickly I didn't even know." He calmed his tone down. "Okay honey our ticket is going to be expensive because it is so last minute," he was rushing me, and we hadn't even gotten our tickets yet. Hopefully he would offer to pay. He had come up with this idea, but he had yet to say who was funding this trip. Yes, I had a millions in the bank but shit he didn't need to know that, and I wasn't going to act like I had that much money in the bank either. I loved the man, but I would be damn if he knew how much I had in the bank. I wasn't stupid in love not again. "Babe come on now you know I got it." He told me. I smiled I know the hell he did have it. Bruce had money how much I was not sure of. He was an investor, so he had his money invested into different companies. I heard the front door opening downstairs and I knew it was Cedes. "I gotta go Cedes here I will call you when I am on my ways to the airport." We hung up. Cedes walked in my room looking beautiful as ever. She had her hair in a black bob, and she had some high waist jeans with a red low-cut shirt. She just radiated with beauty without even trying. Although we had the similar scar on our lip, she hid hers pretty well because of her dark skin. "Damn girl Bruce is on me because you late." I sarcastically stated when she made it up the stairs. She laughed and I did too she knew I did not care about Bruce rushing me. I had a new attitude since the death of Hakeem and Cedes knew I was not letting any man worry me. "Girl Bruce had got his nerves with this last-minute stuff where the kids at anyways?" "In the playroom," I pointed to their room. I had my stuff packed and I already had their things packed too. "I don't see why they going over Quita's house you pay me to watch them." Cedes said and that was the truth. "You don't trust me, do you?" The disappointment was all over her face. I could see the sadness in her eyes. I had never thought that Cedes may have thought I didn't trust her. I did trust her we had become good friends. She was the one who had told me the truth about her and Hakeem. If it was not for her, I would still be in the dark about them having kids together. "Yeah I trust you girl. I just don't want Vanessa to trip on you." I replied and that was the real reason. Vanessa never really acknowledged my kids as her niece and nephew, and we were not at all close. "Fuck her this is my job plus they will feel comfortable here at home" Cedes said. She was telling the truth. Hell, what was I thinking having them leaving home when I paid a Nanny? I paid her a good salary too and she really did not have that many duties. Just some days she had to pick them up and drop them off at school. Most days I did that though if I was not busy. She helped me keep the books for all of my companies. Although Bruce and I had a partnership I was still getting a higher percentage and I still wanted to make sure my numbers were looking good. I couldn't entrust him with that. "You right I will let Chiquita know," I said grabbing my phone. She stopped me. "That is my job too I will let her know you just head on out and get to that man of yours everything will be fine here at the house." For once I took Cedes advice, she was right I was paying her and that was stupid for me not to depend on her to take care of the kids. She had been my Nanny for almost a year, and I had not left the kids with her yet and that was a part of her job description. I guess a part of me really did not trust Cedes because it took Hakeem's death for everything to come out. I remember the first time I saw Cedes, her beauty stood out the most to me. We were at Hakeem's older sister Chiquita's house for dinner. She would not even look at Hakeem, but she looked at me. She was his first girlfriend and his first baby mama. Although I loved Cedes like a sister, I still felt a bit of jealousy. Not because she had Hakeem before me, but because she held the exact same title of baby mama, I thought I was the only baby mama. Now my goals of being a baby mama were dead, I was now a girlfriend Bruce's girlfriend, that was the start of becoming a wife. No more kids were coming out of me and that was a fact. After Deena and all the beatings, I got my tubes tied I was not going to have any more of Hakeem's kids that was for certain and I didn't want anybody else's kids either. I had other dreams besides being a mother I wanted to be a businesswoman and Bruce was making all of that possible. I put some MAC lip gloss on and waited for Bruce. He had decided to pick me up since I told him Cedes was going to stay at the house with the kids. I was sitting in my living room in a daze I had never left the city before and this was going to be my first trip. To think Hakeem had all that money and we did go places, but he never took me out of town. This was going to be my first trip and I was excited but also, I was a little sad. Sad because truth be told I kind of wished that this was Hakeem and I building an empire together instead of Bruce. Hakeem and I had our problems, but I could not help but to miss him. I missed the way he smelled, the way he looked at me, the way we made love. I loved everything about that man and hated everything about him too. It was a win lose situation with us and I was glad I won but deep down I really was sad about how things had to be. I had prepared for the worst outcome with Hakeem, but I never thought it would have come down to his death. I was happy that my misery was over, but I was still in love with what I thought might have been if Hakeem had changed or if I knew how to help him. You can't help wondering about what could have been because it is a mystery. Especially when you love somebody it makes you wonder why they are treating you a certain way. Unfortunately, I found out about Hakeem's own abuse too late, after his death. I think if I would have known the reasons behind the beatings things would have been so much different and I could have helped him instead of hurting him like he had done to me so many times. The blaring of Bruce's horn brought me back to reality. I called up to Cedes, "alright I am gone! Kiss the kids for me I will call you guys later." "Okay honey, have fun on your trip and be safe." She yelled back. I don't know why I was so worried about the kids Cedes was like the sister I never had and I was grateful plus I was going to call Chiquita and let her know that I had left the kids with Cedes and I know that if she touched a hair on their head Chiquita would be all over her ass.

BRUCE

When I hung up the phone for Aniya, I felt like punching the wall. I know she had some damn money and she going to ask me to pay for the trip. The fuck was wrong with her she act like I didn't know she had some fucking money. We hadn't been dating that long. Shit not even six months done went by and this bitch was on some other shit. I knew I had her right where I needed her though because shit, she put me on all of her companies she was stupider than I thought. I put in a little work and then she was putty in my hand. Ha! Too easy! Now I was making this move with myhalf-brother Rashad to expand to Atlanta. I really didn't want to do business with the nigga but whatever I needed this shit to go through. I really did not think that Aniya would be this easy to get too but she proved me wrong. I would wine and dine her and her little kids every now and then and she was open. We would stay up late nights in the office and all I had to tell her was that she was beautiful. No lie Aniya was a beautiful woman. Thick hips and thighs with a pretty face and sexy dick sucking lips what man wouldn't love that, that is what made this opportunity easier. The truth was although she was beautiful, she was not the bitch for me I had a woman. Teresa was my woman. Nice tanned skin, blonde hair, green eyes, and she was made like a Barbie. She was going to be the bitch that I married. Shit if Aniya had that thought in her head she might as well get it out of her head. I was using the bitch and she didn't know it. I just had to work a bit harder so that I could get her to sign all the companies over to me. My phone rung and I knew it was that hoe Italy. "Hello!" I yelled into the phone her voice irritated me. "Are you still coming?" She asked in her thick accent. "Yeah my bitch coming with me," I had to let her know to not make it noticeable that we were fucking every now and then. "Whatever." She hung up the phone. Hoes be so stupid that is why I couldn't even deal with no one but my baby Teresa she was the only woman I loved, and no one even knew about her she was my little secret. She knew about the "relationship" with Aniya and she gave me no problems. She knew her man was about his money. No monkey business.

Chapter Two

BRUCE

W e arrived at the airport and we had to wait three hours do you believe that shit THREE FUCKING HOURS! I didn't purchase the tickets I was really hoping that Aniya wouldn't mind paying but the bitch fooled me. She stayed seated like she was waiting on something while I went up to the desk. Once I paid for the tickets, I sat down to explain to Aniya about my half-brother Rashad who wasn't shit. I know I was doing this business with my brother, but I had nothing but hatred for the muthafucka. I had four siblings that was not including Rashad. Rashad hoe of a mother had stolen my Dad Brandon from my mom. I mean come on my father loved me he named me with a B just like his name. Rashad what kind of stupid ass name was that? My mother knew about Rashad's mother Renee, but the bitch was evil or something she suckered my father into leaving my mother. I really think the bitch put her period blood in his spaghetti one day. They say that is how women make men fall in love I don't know how true that is, but I am sure that bitch Renee did some type of voodoo shit like that. My mother Chelsea died a couple of years ago may she rest in peace. I mean my Mama wasn't lonely or no shit like that because she did remarry Larry my stepfather. Larry was rich as fuck and he taught me every fucking thing I knew. I had invested in all types of businesses when I was about twenty- two years old. Over the last two years those investments have not been doing well. That is why I set it up where I was going to buy Aniya's companies but at the last minute, I told her we should share. That way I only invested a little bit of money and still made money. No lie these months have been great the money from her companies have been paying my bills, but I wanted it all and I was going to get it all. Larry had cut me off from money and he moved away. My thoughts are he went to Florida and moved in with his daughter. Whatever the case is that muthafucka left me high and dry and now I had to fend for myself. I know Aniya had kids but shit a con was a con and she was the victim.

ANIYA

Damn Bruce needed to shut the fuck up! All he talked about was how spoiled Rashad was. He talked about how every summer when Rashad would come to visit, he would have better clothes then him and his brothers and sisters. I was thinking well hell that was your mama and Larry fault, but I would just listen. He and Rashad had fights and a lot of times Bruce and his brothers Rick and Tyler would jump on Rashad, so his mother stopped letting him come to visit. Rick and Tyler were older than Bruce and his sister Rebecca was one year younger than him and Elise was about nineteen. Rashad was a couple of years older than Bruce, so I guess he was about thirty-four, so his father was cheating on his mother. Eventually the back and forth between women had become too much and Brandon chose Renee and left Chelsea. That was all Bruce talked about when Rashad's name was brought up but for some reason, he trusted him to help expand. Well I don't think he really trusted him I think that he was the only person he knew to help expand so he was taking advantage of the opportunity. "Honey when you meet Rashad and his whore of a mother just be respectful. I know they are some dirty people but just remember that everybody cannot be as respectable as you and me." Brue advised me. I just nodded my head. What the hell he thought I was going to go in there and say? Oh, hello Rashad and your whore of a mother Renee. Your trifling ass stole my man's daddy. I mean come on he, act like I didn't know how to act or like I was some ghetto hood rat. I was noticing that a lot lately with Bruce. Before we would go places, he would say, "And don't call out the waiter or waitress name when we go to this restaurant this is not Applebee's this is a real nice restaurant." At first, I would laugh and take it as a joke and be like boy you crazy but now I was starting to wonder. Did he really think I was an ignorant ghetto black chick? Don't get me wrong everyone has their ghetto side to them hell he did something's that I felt was ghetto, but I did not judge. I had never shown Bruce that I could be ghetto, so it baffled me when he said those things out of the blue. One day we were in the grocery store and the line was super long. I turned my face up because who wants to want in a long line. Bruce on the other hand was outright ignorant with it when he saw the line and turned red, "damn they only got one cash register open!" He said it so loud he embarrassed me. People were looking at me and him. I tried to shut him up. "Well honey it is late at night they probably don't have anyone that is able to work." "Naw these muthafuckas need to do some more hiring!" He growled. I looked at him in utter shock this white boy with the prettiest green eyes had a nasty mouth. I would have never guessed that Bruce could talk like that. I couldn't do anything but laugh to try to shake off my embarrassment. Not only that but everyone in the store was black and here I was a black woman with a white man and he was acting like that. It was bad enough people stared at us and whispered things about us when we walked past but Bruce was just acting so ignorant. People always looked at mixed couples and we were no different. Black men looked at him and thought how did he get that fine sister. While white men thought what he is doing with her? The women were out right cruel when it came to it because they would be loud with their remarks. White women would say how fat I am while black women would say he was my trick no matter what people said it all hurt the same. It got to the point that I didn't even want to go places just because of how people would look at us. I was a proud black woman, but I can't lie those people made me feel uncomfortable. I called and checked on the kids to make sure Cedes had fed them. She had decided to have her kids come stay the weekend at my house too and I was fine with that. She needed the break from Vanessa I did not know what she was going to do about their little problem. Chiquita and I had gotten cool after we had the sit down and she told me about their childhood, and I thought I could confide in her about Cedes and Vanessa's problems. She told me straight up, "I know Vanessa looks like a man, but she bleed once a month just like we do Cedes better beat her ass." And to be honest I had to agree. Cedes was acting too timid like she was so afraid of Vanessa. I mean she had her own money and like Chiquita said Vanessa was a woman also she better fight her back which she say she was, but she always came out beat up. My situation was different, and I had to fight back, and Hakeem was a man a strong man at that. I beat him and overcame my fear hell I was already getting beat on I had nothing else to do but get killed or do the killing and I am above ground while he is six feet deep. On the outside I make it seem so easy, but truth be told I missed Hakeem more than I was expecting. I felt guilty a lot when I stared in my son's Malcolm's eyes because he looked so much like his father. Then I take a step back and smile because I know that Hakeem suffered, and I had killed him, but I had also ended his suffering. I know he loved me, but I also knew that he could never love me right and for that he would always be torn between beating me and not beating me. That is what made me get through every day by knowing that yes, I was in the wrong, but I had also helped ease his pain. We finally got on the plane and I was exhausted! Waiting and thinking make you exhausted without you even knowing. I put my headphones on and listened to my Pandora. As soon as it came on Jagged Edge's "Walked Outta Heaven" came on and I sat back closed my eyes and reminisced about my love with Hakeem. I don't know why I always thought about him, but he was always on my mind or in the back of my mind. I knew that Hakeem was the man for me the first time we made love. He did something to me. He made my body scream. Bruce and I had sex and it was nothing like Hakeem. Yes, Bruce took his time and he was an okay sex partner. I missed the way that Hakeem's sexy big lips would kiss the nape of my neck. Damn chills ran down my back. I had to stop thinking about this man, that man, my man. I find myself thinking about Hakeem even when Bruce is giving me head. Bruce is sensual, while Hakeem is nasty. The way he would grab my legs and pull me close to him and I swear you would think he was eating his fruits and vegetables. Oh, I loved that man and everything about him so why did I kill him? As soon as that thought popped in my head it went away. I did not kill him he killed himself. He had been beating me for five years so why should I be guilty, why should I feel this way? Duh, I knew the answer to that I had a conscience. I had so much love for that man that although I know I had to do what I needed to do it still did not change the fact that I had purposely taken a life, but as a mother I would do anything for my children even if it meant killing their father. That hour and forty minutes flew by so fast hell our wait at the airport was longer than the actual trip that was Bruce's fault for not planning ahead. We were exiting the plane and I bumped into this guy and he smelled so good. He smelled like Hakeem, fresh Irish Spring. I looked up and my heart skipped a beat. He was gorgeous. He was light skinned just like Hakeem but he had brown eyes and he had braids in his hair, but I knew a look alike and he was definitely gorgeous just like my baby's daddy. "My bad lil mama," he smiled, and his six gold teeth shined. Yes! He was fine. "It's okay you good." I said and he grabbed my arm. It sent chills up my body. "What's your name?" He asked and that is when Bruce intervened. "My lady that's her name," Bruce sneered. He snatched my arm and pulled me along. I wanted so badly to look back, but I knew that would have been disrespectful. We retrieved our bags and that fine dude was coming to retrieve his bags also. It was crowded but he made sure he walked past me, and I smiled. He was gorgeous and although he was close to me, he didn't even look my way. I know he purposely wanted to be near me just to see how I would respond to his presence. Damn Bruce! I wanted to grab this man and make him mine and pretend that he was Hakeem all over again. As we were walking out of the airport the sun hit me and it felt so good. It was April in Wisconsin and it was cold as hell. I guess that is what happens when you get out and explore you get to see the different climates because it had definitely taken me by surprise. Sometimes I wondered to myself why I did not explore and get out and date. It did take me a while to date Bruce, but he was pursuing me so much that I really did not have time to explore other options. I was locked away with Hakeem and after that I was too afraid to let people in hell it took Bruce a while to get through, but he did. I always wondered well not always but sometimes I wondered why I picked Bruce why didn't I pick someone else? The truth was he was the only man giving me the time of day. As we exited the airport there stood another fine man in front of me. My kitty immediately got wet. Did all the men look this good in Atlanta? He was six two with light buttermilk skin. You could tell he was mixed, and he had the sides of his hair cut into a fade, but the top was curly. He had on a white

Polo shirt and he had on some sunglasses and I wanted to see his eyes. It was lust at first sight. His body was built just like Nelly and I knew he was a God. He took off his glasses and those gray eyes pierced into my eyes and we locked for just a second before I snapped back into reality. "C' mon babe my brother is on time for once." Bruce said and I was mad hell he was about to lead me away from my future husband but to my surprise he led me right to him. This man was still staring at me and I felt dirty like I was not looking cute enough. I don't know where in the hell Bruce's brother was, but it was only that fine man that I saw. To my disbelief we walked right up to that caramel God. "Babe this is my brother Rashad, Rashad this is my lady Niya." I was in awe. This fine ass man was his brother. I was expecting a handsome man but not a handsome black man. He reached his hand out to shake mine I didn't know what to say so I just smiled and when our hands touched, I knew the feeling was mutual. He wanted me just as bad as I wanted him. I had never felt this before. Even when I had met Hakeem, I liked him, but this was something like a fairy tale. It was not until Hakeem and I had sex that I really was sprung on him, but this man had only looked at me and I wanted to be his one and only.

Chapter Three
ANIYA

My heart was racing as I thought about Rashad throwing me up against a wall. I had to shake my thoughts away he was my boyfriend's brother. I could understand why Bruce was so upset and jealous now. Rashad was fine as hell. As we made it to the car Rashad smiled at me and I blushed. "Pretty ladies should not carry their own suitcase," we smiled at each other. As the sun hit his grey eyes, I thought to myself damn I am in love. Bruce must have felt the vibes because he put his arm around my neck. "Damn what you trying to do push up on my lady?" Rashad didn't reply he just grabbed the suitcase from me and put it in the back of his Hummer. I climbed in the backseat. I really wanted to sit in the front next to Rashad's sexy ass. It was nice in his car and it smelled good like lilac. As we pulled off from the airport Bruce and Rashad started to converse. I was in a daze as I stared at Rashad's beautiful profile. The man was fine his goatee around his mouth was extra sexy and the way his lips moved when he talked. Damn I needed to take a cold shower when I got to his house. He said something and it must have been for me because I saw him look in his rearview mirror at me and Bruce had turned around. "What honey?" I asked. I needed to pull myself together I was acting crazy. This man was Bruce's brother the brother that he hated might I add. "Bro here said do you want to get in the pool when you get to his house?" Bruce asked the question. "I didn't bring any swimming clothes." Damn I wish I had so I could show this body off to Rashad. I was proud of my size and I had ass and hips for days and my titties still was sitting pretty. I wanted to show this BBW body off. "That's okay my friend will hook you up she at the house making some food right now." Rashad said and although that baritone voice turned me on the words that came out of his mouth pissed me off. Friend? Yeah, I knew what that shit meant somebody he was fucking with benefits. "Is that right we will see," was my reply and I meant that. Bruce might have thought that I was talking about swimming but the look I gave Rashad and the look he gave me as he glanced in his rearview, he knew what I meant. Although it may have sounded innocent enough Rashad knew I wanted him, and I knew that he wanted me too. We pulled up to a beautiful brick house and I fell in love. It was not big it was a perfect family house though. He lived in a nice neighborhood in Atlanta from what I could tell. I did not know the area but from what I could see it was nice. We had to walk to the back of house and there was a pool. The water looked about 5 feet and was a decent size. Sitting in the pool sat a beautiful brown-skinned woman. She had her lace front wig in a bun ponytail so that it would not get wet and her brown face was cute with just a splash of makeup. "Italy this Bruce my brother and his lady Niya," he introduced us as we walked up to her by the poolside. "You think that you could find her something to wear to swim in?" She got out of the pool and her body was gorgeous. She was top heavy, and she really was not as big as I thought. She had no stomach and her legs were small. She had a Barbie doll figure. I think her boobs were fake they were too perfect. Those brown titties sat up just right and she did not have a bra on. I examined them they were at least a DDD. "Yes of course," she said with an accent I never heard. She looked black but I think that she had to be some type of Hispanic or something. She grabbed my hand and led me inside. I tried to grab my suitcase, but Rashad intervened. "I will put it up for you." He said in a seductive tone or maybe it was me that was just fantasizing he said it in a flirtatious way. No! Forget that he wanted me. It was not just the way that he talked it was also the look in his eyes that let me know he wanted me. We walked in the kitchen and hurried to a little room next to the kitchen. The kitchen was a nice size that had a white wooden table with four chairs. It smelled good in the kitchen and I had to wonder if this brown skinned cutie could compete with me in the kitchen. You know what they say about food being the key to a man's heart. As I looked at Italy, I was not sure that I would be able to fit in any of her clothes. She was top heavy, and I was bottom heavy. "I have the perfect outfit for you," she grabbed a colorful swimsuit. It was cute it was high waist bottoms and the top had some strings dangling from it. It was cute and perfect enough for me to hide my little gut and show off all my other assets. "Damn I thought you would not have my size clothes in here." I admitted to her. "I sell clothes, so I always have different sizes, but this is free to you." She said in her accent. I was happy that I had something to wear I dismissed her so that I could get dressed. It took me a while to get dressed I had to look extra cute for Rashad. I was taking my time to make a grand entrance. As I looked outside, I saw that the sun was setting. I really did not want to get wet then, but I did want to show off my figure in that swimsuit. I had heard them come in the kitchen. Rashad was going to see me in this swimsuit whether I was going to the pool or not. I did a last once over of myself and walked into the kitchen. I didn't give a fuck about Bruce's reaction I wanted to see how Rashad was going to respond to me. I looked over at him, he did a long head to toe look at me and I couldn't help but smile. I know it was worth the wait I could tell by the look in his eyes that he was enjoying the view. "Damn girl what took you so long? It's cold now we not going swimming," Bruce rudely said to me. That was the thing about this weather down south it would be hot as hell during the day and then the temperature would cool down at night. That is what Bruce had told me, but Rashad had a solution for that problem. Once again Rashad intervened, "naw that won't be necessary I got a hot tub too. You ladies can go enjoy." He said. I smiled I liked that idea, but I wanted Rashad to come too. I had not said much since we got there so I just simply looked at Italy to see if she game.

She stood up and that let me know that she was game too. She led me to the hot tub, and I noticed that Italy did have a little butt on her, but it was not as big as mine. I know that Rashad was watching me walk away and just to give myself clarification I turned around to take a glance and he was concentrating on this ass. I put a little swivel in my hips to make sure my cheeks jiggled. We got our bodies in the hot tub and the warm water was like a piece of heaven. We sat in silence for the longest before I started to feel uncomfortable. I sparked up a conversation to pass time and to be quite frank to be nosey as well. "So how long you and Rashad been dating?" I asked being nosey as hell. "Oh no he is not my boyfriend I am engaged to his brother Darien. Rashad and I just keep each other company." She said and yes company is okay but the way she said it sounded more like they were fuck buddies. "Oh, okay do Darien know you guys keep each other company?" I asked sarcastically. Italy nodded her head. "Yes of course. He does not mind he rather his brother keep me company than another man." "So why do he think that is okay?" I wanted to know that shit just sounded crazy. I had been through some things when it came to the situation with James and my Mother, but she was okay with having sex with two men that were brothers. Who was I too judge though because I was contemplating on having sex with Rashad myself, he was too sexy and very hard to resist and I to be honest I wanted to insist that he had sex with me. "Because Darien has been in jail for the last three years and I have been lonely, and he knows it, so Rashad keeps me company." She said it like it was that simple. So, Rashad was single I was guessing. No sane woman would dare allow their man to be banging another woman. "Why you ask so many questions about Rashad?" She looked at me with her little slanted eyes. "Girl I am just nosey." We laughed. Yes, I was being nosey, but I had good reasons I wanted Rashad. I knew I should have kept things platonic between Bruce and I. But hell, after not having sex and being lonely for a year and a couple of months then you would have jumped his bones too. Bruce was a very attractive man with his green eyes and brown hair. He was a bit muscular and he kept himself smelling and looking good whenever I saw him. It was a late night and Bruce and I was in his office. His office was downtown, and he paid next to nothing for the rent. It was mostly for show if you ask me because Cedes and I kept the books of the companies in my home office. On Saturdays just to keep each other company we would link up and go back and discuss the work week and I would give him a report of the accounts. He always was good company too he kept me laughing. We had a couple of drinks that night and we were playing some Usher in the background and I must admit he was looking good that night. We always had a little wine to set the mood because we had some long nights when it came to handling business. The moon was shining through the blinds and the city looked beautiful from the view I could see. I had on some tight blue jeans that hugged my ass right with a sweater. My ass always looked fat in jeans and that was my best asset besides my pretty face. Bruce had on a long sleeve blue shirt with some black slacks. The slightest thing was making me horny and I knew that tonight was going to be the night. The way he was laughing made me wet. The way he was brushing his hand against mine was making my nipples hard. The way he smiled was making me think all types of bad but good thoughts. We were done and it was one o'clock in the morning and we were heading out the door. After hours of flirting with each other we had not initiated anything sexual, but we were about to leave, and Bruce brushed up against my butt and it was on. I turned around and kissed him and as he pushed his tongue down my throat, I pushed him towards his desk. Fuck playing around any longer I needed some dick that Magic Bullet was just not working anymore. He fucked me so good on top of that desk that night and if anybody in the building was working late, I was sure they had heard me. I did not think that sex with him would be so good, but it was great the first time. The first time is usually always good. We had already become a couple after the first time and that was a bummer because the second time was not all that good. Bruce was an okay lover, but he was nothing compared to Hakeem and I bet he had nothing on his brother Rashad. You could tell just by the look of Rashad that he had some good loving inside of him. I knew he did if he was able to sleep with his brother's fiancé, I know he was keeping her satisfied and I wanted some of the action. We chatted for a while and I learned that Italy was a Dominican. She was gorgeous, she was a stripper and one of her tricks had bought her boobies for her. Being a stripper was an interesting lifestyle she told me about all the girls in the club and all the drama. She had me laughing so hard I could barely breath those girls were crazy. She talked about the fights and the way that the women would freshen up she said that sometimes some of the women stank. She did not have just one strip club that she worked at she got requested to go to many different clubs. So, this was the type of shit Bruce and I was going to deal with once we opened our strip club, sounded interesting. Italy had been stripping for most of her life she was twenty-five and was making some good dough because men liked her exotic look. Rashad called for us to come in the house to eat. He had set his dining room table for four. It was cute and I loved the way he kept his house so clean. Bruce on the other hand had to hire a maid because he was such a slob. I remember when the maid Yolanda quit. He said that she was stealing, and she caught an attitude with him when he asked her. I did not believe that though I had talked with Yolanda a lot when I came by and she did not seem like a thief. I think Bruce tried to hit on her and she rejected him, and he fired her. Yolanda was a beautiful girl. She was brown skinned with a big butt and a flat stomach. She wore her real hair in a shoulder length wrap with burgundy highlights. She had small eyes and looked kind of Asian, but she was all black. Bruce didn't know but I kept in touch with Yolanda. She told me that she didn't know why Bruce had fired her. I think she just didn't want to hurt my feelings and expose Bruce. I sort of felt liked Bruce had a different side of him that I did not know about, but all things would surface. Rashad and Italy had prepared some chicken alfredo, asparagus, and some garlic bread. Rashad had popped open a bottle of champagne. "Before we eat, I just want to make a toast to my new business partners" he held up his glass "to Niya and Bruce may our relationship be long lasting." We drank and ate, and I must admit the food was really good. "So Niya how long have you and my brother been dating?" Rashad asked while putting some asparagus in his mouth. Damn he was sexy that even him eating asparagus looked good. "A couple of months," I said after I had swallowed what was in my mouth. "Oh, okay I was surprised I didn't know Bruce liked black chicks." Rashad said and looked at Bruce. Bruce was red for some reason. I knew I was the first black chick Bruce had dated but I don't see how that is a surprise when their Dad liked black women apparently. Guess I was the first black woman to give him a chance. "I guess like father like son," Rashad and I laughed. Bruce did not think my joke was funny. "Well you know what they say pussy is pussy." He said with a smug attitude. I looked at him and I was throwing daggers with my eyes. That right there was rude. I could not believe he would say something like that in front of them and I had just met them. Italy decided to change the subject I guess because the air was getting very thick in there. I was mad as hell how dare he say that. "So, what do you guys plan to name the club?" She asked but I was still on the rude comment that Bruce made. "All I am to you is pussy?" I was passed mad. How dare he in embarrass me in front of people that I do not know how dare he embarrass me in front of his fine brother. That was the real reason I was so hot. "Let us not get into this right now" he answered. His tone let me know that he wanted to curse me out. I had just made a joke and he was taking it too far. His green eyes were squinted, and you could tell he was daring me to challenge him. "You know what you are absolutely right" I turned to Rashad "is there any hotels that you know around here because one thing I will not take is disrespect." That right there sent Bruce through the roof. "Go then! I don't need you!" He got up and yelled at me. I don't know what came over him. He was usually a sweet guy maybe it was the Champagne. He was raising his voice something he rarely did. Was he trying to prove a point to his brother because he was really acting out today and it was very unattractive. "Aye bro calm down!" Rashad said. I looked at Bruce and I wish he would try to hit me because I was going to lay him right on his back. I was still doing my kickboxing with Chance and I was not afraid to do what I had to do. I stood up and got in Bruce's face. I was going to say something to him, but I didn't I looked in his eyes and I knew that Bruce meant no harm. He had never talked to me like this before and I really did not know why he was being so offensive and uncaring, but this was not the man I was dating. "Rashad where is our room I am just going to lie down." I looked over at Bruce and he looked overjoyed. I knew that it was not because I was staying but because I had coward in front of his brother, and he felt like he had the upper hand. He had told me he did not need me and by me staying I showed him that I did need him. Truth be told I only stayed because I still wanted to be near Rashid and also because business was business, I just needed to rethink my business partner. If he was going to keep acting like this, I was going to have to get rid of him. I had taken so many years of disrespect from Hakeem I did not think that I could endure a second of disrespect again.

RASHAD

Man, as soon as I saw Aniya's fine ass, I wanted to beat Bruce's ass and take her down. One thing about me I loved a big fine sexy ass woman I didn't think they made them like that up North, but I was mistaken. She was everything I wanted in a woman. Juanita, Jymie, Clara, shit and the rest of them bitches they had to go because I wanted Aniya. Bruce wasn't shit to me. I just needed his business advice. He jumped at the chance to go in business with me. I was skeptical but my brother Darien said it wouldn't hurt nothing to give him a little percentage. We had been working hard to get this business started. I was ready to get out the game and taking over this strip club from my plug Mr. Richards was just the path that I needed to take. I wanted to see what Ms. Aniya was about though. The bitch Italy was getting on my nerves the entire time before they came. She was acting like she was fucking Bruce or something. She was taking drugs and money to the jail for my brother Darien while he did his time. I missed my big bro like a muthafucka, and I could not wait for him to touch down and cause hell. My brother, my father, and my mother and sisters were everything to me. Especially Rebecca, I couldn't believe I was going through with this business deal with Bruce after all the pain he put my family through. I didn't look at his punk ass as family him or his brothers fuck them. My father wasn't mad when I told him, but my mother was pissed the fuck off when I told her I was doing business with Bruce. I had waited until last night to tell her what I was doing. "Rashad you'se a stupid muthafucka to be fucking with that boy." I started laughing because my Mama always told the truth

"Ma don't trip I got this." I could imagine her rolling her eyes "have you put any thought into what your father suggested?" I had but I just didn't know where to start. The dope game had changed but shit it was my time to shine in the underworld too. "Yeah as soon as I get enough money then we going hard." I told her. "Good okay son love you I will talk to you later." Moms was a trip and she was going to have to wait for me to get this strip club business up and running so that I could get Mr. Richards trust again and see what was going on with him I mean from what I was hearing the nigga was under investigation. I didn't know how true that was, but I wasn't about to play stupid and act like I wasn't aware of the allegations.

Chapter Four

ANIYA

Rashad guided me to our room that was on the second floor. He had pictures going up his steps of what looked to be his mother. I stopped and looked at her. She was a beautiful woman even from the pictures you could tell that she was graceful. She had on red lipstick and although she was up in age her beauty was so youthful. I hoped to be blessed like that when I got older. My mother was a pretty woman her character was not pretty but the way she looked made everyone stop and stare. I missed my mother sometimes I wish things would have been different between us, but it was what it was. She had decided to allow her boyfriend to rape and abuse me for her satisfaction of drugs. I never knew my mother was on drugs because I never really paid attention to her plus she was a functioning drug addict. Things were never what they seemed, but she was on drugs and she let that ruin our relationship. There were so many things that I wanted to ask her that I needed answered. Maybe I would get the answers I needed when I was dead. "That's my mother," he said I turned and looked at his curly hair and pretty smile. This man was beautiful I could tell why Bruce did not like him. Hell, you would be jealous too if your Dad ran off and made something as beautiful as him. From the top of his gorgeous hair he was like a God that was down here on Earth and I definitely felt blessed to be in his presence. "She is beautiful," I smiled and started walking up the stairs in front of him. I made sure to swivel my hips a little because I know he was watching and loving the view. When we got to the top of the stairs, I waited for him to lead the way, but I made sure that he brushed up against my butt as he moved to lead me. He walked me to the room in the middle of the hallway. "That's the bathroom right there if you want to take a shower." He pointed to the door on my left. "Okay that must be your room?" I questioned and pointed to the opposite side of the hallway where there was one door. "Yeah I let Italy sleep in there you know make her a little more comfortable. If you need me I am right next door to you. I sleep in that room." Italy had told me that they were sleeping together I presume that is only when they get lonely. I liked Rashad he was handsome, and I really did not care that he was having sex with his brother's fiancé. It said a great deal about his character but at that moment that was not my concern. Bruce had made me feel some type of way and as a way of getting back at him I was going to show Rashad that I was my own woman plus he was fine, and I wanted to kiss him. I went in for the kiss and it was like time stopped. At first, he was not kissing me back, but I pushed my body towards him and grabbed him around his head and he followed suit. He broke the kiss and I was mad. That kiss had me in another time zone and he had abruptly brought me back to time. "You can't be doing that shit girl." He said but I put my hand on the print of his pants and he was on hard, so I knew I had turned him on. He backed away. "Whatever Rashad look I want you and hell if you can be fucking you brother's fiancé then you should be willing to fuck your other brother's girlfriend." He looked at me like I was crazy. Maybe I was coming on too strong. "Fucking who's fiancé? I don't know what you talking about!" He told me, "you got me fucked up." He turned and left. I stood there feeling like an idiot. Damn I had made a complete fool of myself. I went to the bathroom and looked at myself in the mirror. I took a long hard look at myself. Who was I becoming? I was once a broken woman that would not even think about cheating on my abusive baby daddy but here, I was trying to have sex with my boyfriend's brother. Bruce was an okay guy. On occasion he did get smart with me and belittle me, but he was still nothing like Hakeem. Hakeem would belittle me and beat my ass and I would not dare cheat on him I would not dare look at another man. Here Bruce was allowing me into his world and all I could do was be a slut and try and sleep with his brother. Yes, Rashad was handsome, but I still had no right to kiss him and throw myself at him. I had made a mistake and I was hoping that Rashad did not tell Bruce. If he told Bruce it would be an end to everything I wanted. I ran some hot bath water and got my pajamas. Once the tub was ready slipped my tired body into the tub. It had been a long day and it was going to be an even longer weekend. Since I had kissed Rashad those images kept popping in my head and although I knew it was wrong that kiss made me want him even more. I could not explain it was like although he was forbidden fruit, I still wanted to sink my teeth in that apple. I had spent enough time in the bath, and I needed to get out before I turned into a raisin. I had heard everyone go into their own separate bedrooms. I had my shorts on with my wife beater and I did not have on a bra or panties that's how I liked to sleep. I went into the room I was going to share with Bruce, and he was not in there. I was stunned where could he be, I thought? I went to the room on the other side of the steps to ask Italy since I did not want to bother Rashad after I made an ass out of myself. You know what it was a bit of Italy's fault for lying to me and making me think that Rashad was that type of man. She sat in my face and told me that Rashad was sleeping with her. I knew what it was she wanted Rashad just like I did. She probably told me that so I would not pursue Rashad, but she did not have to worry about that I had made a mistake kissing him and that would not happen again. Her door was open. Rashad's room was nice it had a big king-sized bed in there with a blue comforter with a tiger in the middle. He had a flat screen on the wall mounted with surround sound. He even had a stripper pole that let me know he was a freak. I was game for that. I would dance and shake my ass for Hakeem all the time. He loved it he loved everything about me and hated it just the same. Just like me I loved everything about Hakeem and hated everything just the same. I pushed Hakeem out of my head because whenever I thought about him, I would always think about his death. His death which was my fault and also his fault, although I had done the deed, he had provoked me. I had to keep reminding myself that I had to do what I had to do, and that Hakeem was in a better place. Italy was in the bathroom I could hear the shower running. I decided to go to Rashad's room to see if he knew where Bruce was. I walked back to the other side of the hallway. His door was cracked, and I was just about to knock when I heard him talking on the phone. "Yeah he in the hot tub," the other person must have been talking because he had stopped talking then he started back again. "Yeah nigga she bad with a fat ass and she kissed me. I should have fucked her just because." He stopped and let the other person talk. "I know that nigga really don't like me but shit I am trying to get this money to start up the club fuck him." So, Rashad knew Bruce did not like him and he thought that I was bad. Shit he sure should have fucked me because I was ready. I hurried on back to my room and started devising a plan. I could not pass up this opportunity to be with Rashad yes Bruce was a nice guy, but I wanted Rashad and I knew that he wanted me too. When Bruce came in an hour later, I was pretending to be sleep. I did not want to talk to him, and I did not want him to say anything to me.

To my surprise he thought that he was going to wake me up to have sex. He rubbed his dick against my ass. I was livid how dare he think that he was going to disrespect me and try to get some he had me all the way fucked up. I kindly got up and went downstairs. I heard the television on in the living room and was shocked to see Rashad's sexy ass sitting in there watching television. He did not have his shirt on, and he had a tattoo with is mom name on his chest. He was sexy and I wanted him even more. I went and sat down next to him. "I just want to say I am sorry about earlier." I looked at him and his sexy face damn I just wanted to kiss him again. I would have too if I wasn't so scared of rejection and the fact that Bruce may come downstairs. "It's cool I know how it can be sometimes but why do you think that I am sleeping with Italy?" "Because she told me that she said that she was engaged to your brother and he was in jail for three years. She said since he was in jail he told her that you guys could have sex so that she would not sleep with no one else." I said fuck it she had lied to me and had me making a fool of myself shit I was gone confess. He started laughing, "that Italy boy she is something serious." That was all he said. I looked at him. "We okay right?" I asked him. He looked intensely at me. My pussy got so wet you would have thought we were making love. His eyes just did something to me he was so attractive to me. It was not just how he looked it was also something else I knew that he had a good personality too I could tell. "Come with me." He grabbed my hand and I went without any hesitation. We went in the back by the pool. It was dark and he pulled me on the side of the house where we could not be seen. "You have to be quiet," he said as he pushed my body against the side of the house. I did not know what was about to happen but he kissed me and I kissed him back. We were in a long sloppy wet kiss and like the McDonalds slogan I was loving it. He grabbed at my shorts and started pulling them down. He touched my vagina. "Just how I like it naked" he said. He stopped kissing my mouth and started kissing my neck. I was so hot and horny I just wanted him to stick it in, but he had other ideas. He put his tongue on the opening of my vagina and licked it. Then he opened it up and started sucking on it like it was a nipple. I was standing on the wall of the house and he was on his knees. I was trying to be quiet, but it was so damn good. He knew what he was doing, and I was in love. He put his tongue in my opening and I let out a loud moan. He did not stop there, and my legs were on top of his shoulders while my body was keeping me up against the wall. He was working his tongue like a blender and it was hitting all my secret spots. I had never had it done like this before and especially not lately. Bruce did not really know what he was doing so I rarely asked him to do it and Hakeem was good, but Rashad was like Frosted Flakes he was grrrrreat! I was screaming too loud and Rashad stopped. I didn't even know if Bruce had fallen asleep and I really didn't care but Rashad was thinking. He put me down and I was still shaking. I had my shorts still around my ankles and I was in pure bliss. He started laughing "pull yourself together girl." I just looked at him and I pulled my shorts up. "Come on." He said. We went back into the living room and started watching television as if nothing had happened. "What you want to watch?" Rashad asked I was still in shock, so I just shrugged my shoulders. "You don't say much do you?" He smiled and my heart melted. He put on Boyz In the Hood and sat next to me. "I don't want you to think differently of me, but I do like you. I can tell you are something special even though you don't like to talk. You know that scar on your face and that pain in your eyes tells me plenty about you. That is what I think is drawing me to you. And for the record I did not smash Italy." He laughed and I laughed too. I did not understand how this man who I had just met could read me so well. Bruce and I had spent well over a year together and he never noticed the sadness in my eyes. If he did, he never brought it up. I know I had done the unthinkable and had killed Hakeem, but it was good reason. He was the man I loved, and I did miss him. Especially at night that was my loneliest time. Every night no matter what I always had someone to hold onto. If Hakeem and I would fight and argue I would go in the kids' room and hold them. Most of the time it would only last a day or so because I would miss Hakeem so much yes, I wanted the beatings to stop but I did not think that missing him would be this hard. As I snuggled up next to Rashad on that couch, I closed my eyes. Hakeem's face popped into the darkness of my mind. My heart grieved for the man I loved, my conscious was guilty.

RASHAD

Aniya's sexy ass came downstairs with those little ass shorts on and that was all she wrote. I had to have her. I mean from the jump I was feeling her, and my brother Darien told me I should go for it. Bruce had cost our family nothing but pain and suffering. Plus, she could be wifey for all I knew. When she walked down the stairs and those titties were perky without a bra I all I wanted to do was eat her up and let me tell you she tasted good as hell. I took her outside on the side of the house. I know that bitch Italy was listening that is why I took her and ate that pussy right outside my bedroom window. I don't know why Italy was so pressed about coming over this weekend. She knew I wasn't going to fuck her so why come over here. When Aniya told me one that Italy told her she was Darien's fiancée that was a lie right there because bro was already married and two that I was fucking her I felt like whooping her ass, but I don't hit women. Aniya was soft as she lay in my lap and watch television with me. Her hazel brown eyes were hypnotizing and from what I could see she was a lost soul looking for love. SHIT! Bruce was not the nigga to give her that I was, but it was going to be up to her to recognize that. I ate that pussy to let her know I was feeling her. Now it was up to Ms. Aniya to decide if she wanted to fuck with a real nigga or a real wigga the choice was hers. But knowing my brother Bruce he was going to fuck up royally as usual and then I was going to swoop in like Prince Charming and get the Princess.

Chapter Five

niya Rashad and I must have fallen asleep on the couch because we were awaken by a shocked and upset Bruce. "What the fuck is going on?" He screamed. It woke me up and I was lying on Rashad's lap. Rashad looked down at me and I looked up at his gray eyes. He still had sleep in his eyes. "Bro it ain't even like that we were down here watching a movie and we must have fallen asleep." I got up off his lap. I was glad he had said something because I was truly at the point where I did not give a fuck. "I thought pussy was pussy," I said to let him to let him know I was still pissed about the comment he made. He sat next to me on the couch and tried to grab my hand. "Niya you know I did not mean

59

that shit. You still mad about that?" He kissed my cheek "Don't be mad at me babe please." He said I looked at him and although I was still mad, and I did not want to be with him I did not know where I stood with Rashad. "Okay Bruce just watch your mouth." I said and got up and started towards the stairs. Huh I was getting tired of him. I know I was getting tired of him because I wanted Rashad, but I really needed to slow my role. I didn't even know where I stood with Rashad and here, I was talking stuff to the man I had been in a relationship with for the past couple of months and besides he was also my business partner. I don't know what Rashad had told Bruce, but he came upstairs and apologized to me. I was happy for that because I really did not want him to press the issue because I did not know what to say to Bruce about why I was sleep on the couch with Rashad. I got in the shower since we were going to talk to the club owner at the strip club that we were trying to buy. My pussy was still throbbing from the licking that Rashad had put on me last night. As the water hit my body, I felt a sensual touch. It was my hands grabbing myself. I felt across my little nipple and they stood to attention. I loved the way my body felt. I moved from my titties to my pussy and I imagined Hakeem at first. I remember when we had a fight over some bullshit.

He wanted me to come get him from work one day and I had my phone off while I was at school. He beat my ass so bad that day I was in the shower crying as blood ran down my leg. He had pushed me on the glass table, and it broke thankfully it had only cut my leg. I was crying so hard and long I could see the hurt in his eyes after he had done it. There were a few times when he would beat me that he would actually look sympathetic and remorseful and that was one of the times. I screamed out in pain and I started crying. He reached out for me and I pulled away. "Baby I am so sorry please let me help you." He said and tried to reach for me again. "No," I said trying to wipe my tears "just get Malcolm to sleep." He had roused him up from the loud crash and he was crying. Malcolm was about one when that happened. I got in the shower to wash away the pain, shame, tears, and blood. I heard the door creep open. "Baby you okay in there?" Hakeem asked while he stood outside the curtain. I was crying so hard and it was uncontrollable. My heart hurt, I hated him and here he was acting like he had not done this shit to me. "No!" I cried out and when I said that he snatched the curtain open. He climbed in the shower with me in his clothes. I will never forget he had on his shoes and everything. He had on an expensive LRG outfit with some brand new

Jordans he had bought, and he got his whole body wet to console me. We sat in the bathtub, I was butt naked and he had his clothes on while the water fell down on us while he held me while I cried. I cried because he had hurt me but here, he was holding me, and it made me feel better. That was Hakeem he was the root of my pain, but he was also the reason for my happiness. I knew it was going to be hard getting over Hakeem but as I was in that bathroom in Atlanta in my boyfriend's brother bathroom, I noticed that I was crying. I was crying from the memory of my baby daddy. The one I had loved the one I had killed. I hadn't cried for almost a year, but I thought about Hakeem more than I liked too. I had to shake him off my mind. I put on my light blue skinny jeans with a pink shirt and my pink pumps with the bow in the front. I was feeling good about myself. I fixed my short hair that I had dyed blonde a month ago in a cute little style where I curled the front a little and put a bang. I put on a little mascara and eyeliner. I decided to wear some pink lip gloss and I was ready. It had taken me an hour and a half, and I had not heard anything the entire time from anyone. I know Bruce was getting dressed so I hope they did not leave me. I went into the room that we were staying in and put my dirty clothes in my suitcase. I walked down the stairs. I did not see anyone in the living room, so I went into the kitchen where they were finishing breakfast. So much was going on that I had forgot that I had not even really eaten dinner. I grabbed a plate and sat down to eat. The chair next to Bruce was open so I sat next to him. He looked at me and smiled. I looked over at Rashad and he was looking at me also I could see the lust in his eyes. Italy was not dressed and was walking around in a robe that little slut was trying to be noticed. Now that I knew she was a liar it kind of pissed me off. After breakfast we headed out to see the owner of the strip club. I guess he was retiring, and he wanted to sell. Al Richards was his name and he was a well-known businessman out in Atlanta. I heard that he was a drug lord also, but I wasn't sure, and I really did not give a damn I wanted him to give us a good price on this club because the price that he had thrown at Rashad was not going to happen. I was under the presumption that we had closed the deal but when I saw that paperwork, I was not having it we needed a better deal. We pulled up at the club that was called "Sugars" ugh I was going to change that. Bruce was dressed nice in a gray suit with a white shirt underneath. Rashad had on a black LRG shirt and he had on some blue LRG shorts with some black Jordans he looked nice, but he looked a bit hood. I watched as he walked and got instantly turned on. It was just something about that Rashad he was something I had never experienced before. Hakeem dressed like the thugs, but he was not a thug he was a businessman. It was something about Rashad that let me know that he was a thug. We walked into the strip club and it looked like a typical strip club and it made me want to change it. I had so many ideas. Al Richards was sitting at the table with another guy. Al was a short Mexican older guy. The guy that was sitting next to him looked familiar. As we got closer to the table, I noticed it was the guy from the plane. I could tell he noticed me and inside I smiled. Look at his fine ass the incarnation of my baby daddy. We made it to them and both gentlemen shook Rashad and Bruce's hand they kissed mine and Hakeem's look alike pulled out my chair.

I could tell Bruce caught that he was the same guy from the airport, and he seemed to have a little attitude. Fuck Bruce we needed to get down to business and I guess they were the people who we were going to negotiate with. Al spoke first, "this here is my nephew Crenshaw," he said, and I looked him over. He was definitely fine and reminded me of my baby daddy especially those sexy lips, they were just like Hakeem. Bruce spoke for us, "this here is my lady and business partner Aniya and you know my brother

Rashad." He said. I don't know why he had to make sure he had to tell people I was his lady. "Okay let's get down to business." Al said he did not have an accent you could tell he was born in America and his family had been Americanized. If I was not sitting in his face, I would have not known that he was a Mexican. He was talking and going in circles trying to hustle us. I did not like him, and he was pissing me off. Rashad was looking like he was bored, and Bruce was sweating for some reason. I could tell that they were new to this. I already knew that Rashad was, but Bruce told me he had other businesses I was starting to think that was a lie. Once he got done giving us his price and his rules I started to speak and Bruce spoke before I could, "that sounds great," Rashad and I looked at him like he was crazy. "No that sounds like some great bullshit if you can excuse my French," I said, and Al smiled while Bruce looked on in shock. Forget that he was not going to hustle us. "So, you feel like we need to pay you full price and we still have to pay taxes plus keep your strippers that work here? First of all, some of them gots to go I saw the books they not making as much as they should, and I want to know why? Do not play us for no fool Mr. Richards. You have been running this business for over ten years and I want to know why you are ready to sell?" He looked at me and I looked at him. He wanted to know what I knew. I knew it all he was in a hole with the bank and he needed to sell everything real fast. He had not been paying his taxes and he was damn near bankrupt. I do not know if he was still in the dope game but if he wasn't, he was going to go back. "You are going to have to excuse her it is that time of the month." Bruce said. This is what I hated about Bruce. He was trying knock me for being a sassy talking businesswoman. He was supposed to be backing me up. He had not even done his homework on this guy and he was ready to sign his name on the dotted line. Yes, we had the money to get the business, but I was damned if we was going to pay the full price. "Shut the hell up Bruce this is a team effort and I will not sign and without my signature there will be no money. That is right Mr. Richards I hold the money." That was a lie Rashad had the money, but I wanted to let him know that I had the brains and the money. This was bad for business I did not want to come off as a bitch, but Bruce was making it hard. He was acting too desperate and I wanted Mr. Richards to know that I was not playing any games that I was not going to settle. Rashad had not said anything I guess because he did not know what to say. Mr. Richards clapped his hands and smiled, "she is brilliant Bruce you keep her on your team. You are right the club is not doing as well as it had before." I looked around, "yes and it need some fixing up. It is a beautiful place so I know you can give me a figure that I can work with and those strippers that ain't worth shit I need names and numbers because I will do the firing." I said matter of fact and the rest would have to prove themselves to me. Strip clubs made a lot of money if it was ran right and I was not about to allow Bruce to fuck up this big deal. Rashad would be running things and he had not said anything, but I could tell he was enjoying the way I talked. I just hope he was the right guy to run this ship. We left the club with a great deal and I had the papers with me so that I could have Susan look them over. When we got in the Hummer of course Bruce had something to say to me. "Damn Niya you have to calm down and not be so ghetto." I was about to say something when Rashad did it for me. "If it was not for her, we would have paid the full price how you hopped on board so fast. Hell, she got him to lower it by fifteen percent and we got rid of those shit talking bad for business ass hoes. He threw you a bad deal and you were ready to take it. Damn what business school you went to?" Damn I did not even know Rashad could talk like that, but it turned me on. "Fuck you muthafucka Larry taught me a lot I just lost my head." He said. "Well you better find it. You know I don't really know about this shit, so I need you to be in this and ready to use your brains." Rashad said and I agreed. I was glad that I had someone on my side. I don't think that Bruce had ever been in a business meeting or his stepfather Larry did all the negotiating. Either that or he was getting played in many of his deals. When we got to the house Bruce told me he needed to talk to me. When we got into the room, I thought he was going to tear into me, but he didn't he broke down and started crying. "Thank you so much baby." He hugged me real tight. "I don't know why I had almost messed that deal up I am so happy to have you." I did not know what to say. I liked Bruce and he treated me nice I needed to give him a chance and stop lusting after his brother. We were building an empire together and I needed to stick with him. I know that he really liked me, but we needed to build that trust. "That is okay baby I am happy to have you too. Was this your first business meeting?" "Yes, usually I have Larry with me, so this was my first time on my own." He said. "Okay baby you have to think before you make deals though honey. And do your research on people who you are dealing with too." I told him. I knew he made lots of money but I never really thought about Larry helping him out so much. "Okay I will do better and I am sorry about all the things that I have been putting you through this weekend. It's just that Rashad makes me a little tense and you are not making it better by saying bullshit." He said. We got up and sat on the bed. I did not see how I was talking bullshit, but I knew how to shut up and agree with my man. I had done it so many times with Hakeem, so I just shut up and allowed Bruce to be the man. "I am sorry baby let us just enjoy the rest of our weekend." I gave him a kiss. I was happy that we made up and all the confusion was over. I was going to try to push Rashad out of my head and move on from the other night. It was going to be difficult to get over a man that sexy and head game that was that excellent.

BRUCE

I cried my fucking eyes out not because I was really sorry but because Aniya had saw me at a weak point. The bitch was smart, and she had done her homework, but I looked stupid in front of Rashad and Mr. Richards. Larry hadn't taught me shit. I followed the man around and begged him to show me stuff, but he never did. Larry always told me that I was evil and a man like me did not deserve to be rich, that was some bullshit. I met Teresa and she gave me ten thousand dollars. Teresa was rich and she assured me that her parents would not approve of me to marry her until I got my money up. I was well on my way when my damn investments started to fail. I quickly pulled out and then I found Aniya. She was my cash cow and she didn't even know it. I had been profiting from her companies, but I needed more. After Aniya fell asleep, I snuck across the hallway to where Italy was sleeping at. The big tittie bitch was pissing me off she knew that I had Aniya coming with me this weekend. I had known Italy for years the bitch was a prostitute and a stripper that I fucked every now and then. I had met her the summer I came to visit my father. They treated me like shit when I came to Atlanta, I ran away one day and decided to explore the city. I was young and I wanted some pussy. I ran up on young Italy who was a prostitute at the time. We became best of friends. After my hospitalization after I came home, we still kept in touch. She called to check up on me she was the only one who checked up on me. That is why my plan was working so well. I was eventually going to take over Rashad's companies also and that is where she came in at. I made sure she got in with Darien. He was my target, but his stupid ass went to jail so now it I turned on my brother Rashad. Darien before he went to jail was the next up and coming kingpin in Atlanta. My father had the title before he was institutionalized. So now the runner up was Rashad and I was going to rob his ass blind. I pushed the door open in a hurry and closed and locked it. Italy was watching television of course naked. I wonder if she was hoping I was Rashad. I walked over to her and pulled my dick out she knew what to do. She crawled on over to me and put her lips on the tip. "Just how I like it baby" I said to her. She knew just what to do. She made sure she rotated her hips so that I could see that ass jiggle. That shit turned me on, and she hadn't even been sucking that long before I bust. She swallowed all my seeds. I got in the bed with her. "Damn Bruce I can't get no dick?" "Nah not tonight." "Hummph so you know Aniya fucked Rashad last night." I snapped my head around so fast because I knew I had heard her wrong. "What the fuck do you mean?" I asked through gritted teeth. Italy looked a bit scared because she knew what I was capable of doing. Italy was also known to be a fucking liar, so she had better been exaggerating. "Well that's what it sounded like I heard her moaning outside." I don't know what else she said because my heart started beating hard and that was all I could hear. Damn not my Aniya I mean I know I was planning on taking the companies from under her, but I still wanted her to be for me. I had to make this shit happen faster that bitch was done for.

Chapter Six

ANIYA

———— ⊶≫≺⊶⊗⊶≻≪⊷ ————

I could not breathe. Hakeem's grip around my neck was tight and I could feel my body becoming lifeless. As I looked into his beautiful eyes I saw the pain, the pain from his father beating him, the pain from his father killing his mother. He was hurting and because of that he hurt me. Hakeem stared deeply into my eyes and our souls interlocked. He released the grip he had around my neck and I fell to the floor. My eyes popped wide open as I looked around the dark room. Bruce was laying next to me, I hated the nightmares that I had about Hakeem. It was hard to shake him. I pushed the covers close to my chin I needed to get some sleep it was our last day in Atlanta and I wanted to enjoy myself. It was Sunday and we had to catch our flight. Bruce and I enjoyed our last night in Atlanta together. Italy had gone out with her friends and I didn't know where Rashad had disappeared too. That night as we shared a laugh over dinner, I kept thinking about the way Rashad had licked my pussy. I thought about the way his tongue circled across my clitoris. I squeezed my legs together as I tried to listen to Bruce. I had to get Rashad out of my head, they were brothers. Rashad drove us to the airport that morning. He had not said anything to me that was sexual or anything. The chemistry between us was undeniable though. When we got to the airport Rashad helped me get my suitcase out of his trunk. Our hands touched and my pussy juiced with wetness. I had to get over him. "I can carry my own bag thanks Rashad." I said as I grabbed my suitcase. The white pants that I had on were fitting me right. I knew as I walked away Rashad was watching. I liked Rashad he was handsome but that one night of pleasure was not enough to make me stop fucking with Bruce. Bruce and I had plans. He worked with me he let me make business decisions that I did not get to make with Hakeem. Bruce made me feel equal like I was just as smart as him. I loved that about Bruce. I was not in love with Bruce, but I loved things about him. Right now, he gave me freedom with the business and most importantly he did not put his hands on me. Bruce was what I needed. When I stepped into my house it was like heaven. Cedes was cooking something that smelled really good. Her boys were sitting in the living room watching television and Malcolm was sitting with his big brothers. I remember when Malcolm found out that Jon-Jon, Junior, and Chris were also his brothers. He was so happy to have big brothers. Deena was the baby and the only girl, and they treated her like a princess. The boys knew Hakeem was their father, but they did not acknowledge him. Whenever he was brought up, they would call him Hakeem. They were the spitting image of him with a little similarities of their mother, but all of his children had his eyes. They were old enough to know the hell that their mother went through and they were also old enough to know that their father acted as if they were nonexistent. Cedes had not told them Hakeem was their father until after he died. She had left him early in their lives, so they really did not remember him. He never said anything to them whenever he saw them, so they were not really missing anything. Hell, none of us were missing anything with Hakeem, he was selfish, abusive, and an ass so we had each other that was all that mattered. I gave all five of my babies a kiss and went in the kitchen. "Hey girl," Cedes said when I walked in. She had on some jogging pants and a red spaghetti strap shirt. "Hey what you cooking?" It smelled so good. "Girl I am cooking some baked chicken, mac and cheese, and string beans nothing too much you know I can barely cook." She laughed. "I know girl but it do smell good." "Yeah my boo been paying for me to get some cooking lessons." This was something new to me I didn't know Vanessa was paying for Cedes to get some cooking lessons. Cedes always did want to learn to cook so I know that meant a lot to her. "Aw Vanessa is sweet for that." I said and Cedes turned her nose up. "Not that bitch! I am talking about Lawrence." I was in shock I did not know they were still fucking around. "What? I thought you were done with him?" It was not something I had asked before but I had just assumed that they were over since she had not mentioned him lately. "I was but I went back, and things are better than ever. He is going to leave Chiquita and be with me when he gets Chiquita to help him establish himself a bit more." I knew Cedes had lost her mind. Chiquita and Lawrence were engaged. Lawrence Sutton was a fine man, tall and gorgeous from head to toe. Lawrence was a damn thug who was trying to change his life and he had met Chiquita. Chiquita was a fashion designer and she did it very well and she knew many famous and important people. Lawrence was using Chiquita to get those individuals on his team because he wanted to start a business. What type of business I did not know but he was using Chiquita to make his way around the rich and famous people. He wanted to build his reputation for whatever business he was trying to start. Chiquita would brag on him whenever I saw her, but she had yet to tell me what kind of business he was starting I guess she would let me know whenever she found out. I personally felt like he was up to no good but who was I too judge and worry hell I had my own life to live. I didn't even know what to say to Cedes if she liked it, I loved it. I went upstairs to take my shower. As I undressed, I looked at my body. It had changed I was still sexy, and my hips and ass was still big, but I had gotten smaller. I loved my shape, my body, everything about myself. I was perfect even the stretch marks and scars on the inside and outside were not enough to tear me down I was strong I had survived. I had killed and I knew that if need be I could do it again and get away with it. As the shower hit my body I started to think about Rashad's soft lips. Oh, I had never had it ate like that before. I loved the way those sexy lips touched the lips of my vagina. He didn't have those juicy lips like Hakeem, but they worked just as wonderful. Every time I thought of Rashad I snapped back to reality because he was forbidden fruit that I had bitten into and I needed to forget about him. I wrapped my body in my peach towel and decided to air dry in my bedroom. April in Wisconsin was nothing like Georgia. It was still cold here and I had the heat on. As I dressed into my black pajamas with the lips and lipstick across them, I looked in the mirror and decided I needed to change my hair. I had always worn short hair styles I was ready for something different. I felt different so I felt the need to change my look. I know Cedes always had her hair done perfectly so I would definitely be asking her who was her beautician. I went downstairs and we ate dinner. I told the kids about how Georgia looked, and Jon-Jon, Chris, and Junior said next time I go they wanted to go. They were old enough so I thought that would be a great idea. We watched movies and Cedes, and the boys left around seven that evening. I do not know why but it just seemed like Cedes did not want to go home. I asked her if she was alright and she said that she was, so I left it alone. I read Malcolm and Deena a bedtime story and we laid in my bed together. I loved my children so much. Malcolm was in the second grade and Deena was in kindergarten and they were both smart and talented.

Deena loved her ballet classes and Malcolm was going for football. I had the best children and I did not need a man to help me raise them. I know I could do it on my own and that was what I was going to do. Bruce did help me out a bit with the kids, but it had been a while since we had done anything together. It was tough doing things on my own, I was grateful to have Chiquita and Cedes. The next day I dropped the kids off at school and headed to my appointment with Princess. Cedes had recommended her and she was nice enough to squeeze me in. She was on the eastside so I rushed through traffic so that I could be on time. It was a bit nippy outside, so I dressed rather warm. I had on some chestnut ankle boots with my black skinny jeans and a black sweater. "Lovely Ladies" was a small shop that looked a bit shabby but Cedes said the lady that was in charge was a damn good hair stylist. I walked in and it was only one person in the building. She was a skinny brown skinned lady. "Hi, I am looking for Princess." I said and since she was the only person in there, I was hoping that she was Princess I did not want to wait for anybody. "She in the bathroom, Princess!" She yelled "somebody out here for you." The girl was sitting in one of the salon chairs. As I waited or Princess, I looked around the salon. It was small but had lots of potential. I knew there was a lot of money in the beauty business. Out came a beautiful brown skinned woman. She was a big boned lady, but her face was beautiful as ever. She had on some lip gloss which made her big lips look sexy. Her big titties was perfectly pushed up and I could tell that bra was very supportive. She had her hair in a natural curly style, and she smiled at me. "Hey you must be Cedes's girl?" I nodded Cedes had called ahead thankfully. "Sit pretty lady and tell me what you might want done to your hair." I sat in a chair near the bathroom. "I just want a change I have always worn a short style. I want some length." "Okay girl well I can put some length, but do you want straight? Curly? Color? Come on give me an idea of what you want." She asked. I told her exactly what I wanted, and she did it. After three hours of being in the shop talking to Princess and Shaneka I was finally done, and I loved the results. She had dyed my Brazilian bundles a red color and wand curled the 24 inches of weave. This was my first time having a sew in. She did an invisible part and I looked in the mirror I looked gorgeous. "Oooh honey this is gorgeous!" I screamed. She was smiling and I had noticed that no one had come into the shop yet. "I know it fits you perfectly. It should stay up a couple of months too. Hit my cell phone and I can do your hair at my house next time.

The shop will be closed by next week." I looked at her and I could see the tears in her eyes. "What do you mean?" I could see the pain in her eyes. "Her son got hit by a car." Shaneka spoke up she looked at Princess. Her voice was soft, "he died and she didn't have any insurance. She is behind on the bills here and it is just too much for her." Princess had found her a seat by this time and the tears had fallen down her eyes. "Oh sweetie do not cry," I got up and grabbed a Kleenex. I wiped the tears from Princess eyes. "This was my dream and I put everything into it." She breathed deeply. "Not only did I lose my child I lost my dream. I had to fire my friends and family who helped me build this place. I can't pay the rent on this shop, hell I can barely pay my rent at the house." "Did you make a lot of money from the shop?" My business mind set in. "Hell, yeah she made a lot girl. She was doing good until this tragedy." Shaneka said. "Okay well this is your lucky day Ms. Princess because you hooked me up and I am a businesswoman I want to help." She looked at me like I was crazy. "Look give me your books so I can go over them and see how I can help and what is your landlord's name?" I asked. "Sheila Pherson." She said as she went in the back, I was guessing to give me her books. She came back with a big black book. I opened it up and was in shock this girl was making money. "How much do she charge for rent?" I asked. From the books it looked like twelve hundred, but I wasn't for sure. "Twelve hundred," she replied. "Okay I can help I will get you out of this hole. Give you some money to fix this place up a bit and I just want a percentage of your profits a month. Can you do that?" I asked and I was hoping she would say yes. Hell, she had her own clients and she was charging her stylists a percentage from their daily makings instead of charging them for a rental booth. She was a smart lady I definitely wanted a piece of the pie. We talked over the details and I called Susan to type up a contract. Princess thanked me and I told her to have a lawyer look over the contract and to get back to me. I had gone into spend some money and in the end, I would be making more money. Yes, I was definitely getting a business sense of mind and I loved it. I sat in my car and took a couple of selfies and sent them to Bruce I hoped he liked them. I did not have anything really to do today so I decided to go to my kids school and surprise them with lunch from McDonalds. As I pulled into the Elementary School, I got a response back from Bruce it said "WTF". I guess he did not like my new look, whatever I looked good. I went into the school and everyone complimented me on my look. That made me feel good because Bruce had me second guessing the way I looked. I had to let that go. One thing about Hakeem he never judged me on my look he always told me I was beautiful and pretty. Hell, why tell someone they are ugly after you just told them they were stupid, did not know how to do shit, was lazy, and so many other insults I guess he had to draw the line somewhere. My kids were so happy when they saw me in the lunchroom with that McDonalds. The teachers allowed them to sit together so that we could eat together. They were both talking and telling me about their day. This was what I loved to make my kids happy and I was glad that I had let the stress of Hakeem go. He was bringing us down with the constant fighting. I wanted my kids to live a happy and healthy childhood so that as adults they would be mentally healthy. I know that as a child I was not raised right and after getting molested by one of my mother's boyfriends I had not really healed from that traumatic event. My mother had allowed so many bad things to happen to me when she was supposed to be protecting me. No parent is perfect though and now that I was a mother, I understood that. The thing about me was I had took my kids father away from them and at the time it was the best thing to do but after finding out so many things about him it might have been better to just get him some help. Now it was too late I had to deal with it. Just like my mother had to deal with the fact that she let me down. I had to deal with the fact that I took their father from them I would forever harbor that guilt.

CEDES

As soon as I came back to Nessa's house I was pissed. She was on my ass like I was fucking Niya. Only if she knew if Niya swung that way I would fuck her for real. Niya had always been pretty to me and I could see why Hakeem loved her so much. One time I had even asked him if we could do a threesome. He smacked me so damn hard he made me remember why I had left him. As of lately Nessa was starting to make me want to leave her. Hakeem put me through some terrible ass whippings and Nessa was up there with him. People would say that she is woman like me but fuck that that bitch was strong. Lawrence was my only escape I just wanted to leave with him. I knew that he was fucking Quita and they were "engaged" but shit once she gave him what he wanted then he was going to be all mine. As I put the kids in the tub and listened to Nessa screaming and talking shit to me, I zoned out. I had been going through this shit since I was fifteen years old, so this was nothing new to me. All three of my boys were in the bed sleep so I decided to get in the tub. Nessa had walked off on me and I was sure she was somewh ere getting a drink. Good that way that bitch could give me some head. I checked my email on my phone and saw that my mother was trying to contact me about my brothers. I did not give a fuck about them jailbirds. I closed my eyes and tried to remember why I fell in love with Nessa. I really did love her she was the one who rescued me from her lunatic of a brother. Hakeem and I had went to high school together and we fell in love. It was something about his sexy gray eyes that pulled me to him. He was smart and funny, but he became crazy. When Nessa found out about him beating me, she told me to leave. Where the fuck was, I going to go? To the damn brothel that my mother called a home HELL NO, so I stayed. Nessa and I was not having sex at first when she moved us out. Over time she just grew on me. We were laying, in bed and she put that mouth on me and I fell in love. Yes, I was still fucking Hakeem because wasn't nothing like a hard dick, but I was not going to leave Nessa. My inability to leave Vanessa had to do with my fear of being beaten on but shit now she was beating on me so why was I still here? I had the money with or without Lawrence and I had a job with Aniya but for some reason

I wanted to make sure Lawrence was going to leave Quita I did not want to be alone. I dried my body off and put on my blue robe. I went in the room and Nessa was sitting on the bed drinking her usual Patron. She smiled at me and I knew she was drunk and wanted some pussy. Nessa was cute as hell to be bald headed and we looked good together. I wanted to feel that gift she called a mouth, so I opened up my robe and let her know that I wanted it too. I sat down on the bed and opened my legs Nessa got up and got on her knees. Lawrence was a good fuck, but Nessa had that magic tongue and I could not get enough. She dived right into my pot of honey with her tongue. "OOOOHHH!" I moaned. No words needed to be exchanged. I opened my legs wider so that she could work like she knew how. She put her tongue on my clitoris and I could feel her tongue ring rub against it, it sent shock waves through my body and that was my first orgasm. OOOOHHH! She inserted her two fingers into my opening, and she did it so gently while she nibbled on my clit. YEE EEE SSS! The other hand she used to rubbed over my ni ppl es. GOOOOOOD LOOOORD! Why was I trying to le ave her? She brought me to that special place at least five more times. I was done and tired and I hadn't ev en done anything but scream and moan. Nessa got up and kissed my lips and I tasted good I must say. "I love you Cedes." "I love you too." I responded as I cuddled next to Nessa. I knew she wasn't stupid she knew I was fucking around behind her back and maybe that was the reason she was hitting me. Maybe if I stopped cheating with Lawrence our relationship would get better.

Chapter Seven
ANIYA

⟶ ⊶⧓⊷ ⟵

It had been a week since the deal with the strip club in Atlanta and Mr. Richards finally got back to us. Susan had gone over the contract and she had made some adjustments and we had been waiting for a call back. Bruce and I had been apart because for some odd reason he did not like my hair, and he was showing how much he hated it. I had come over his house the next day after getting my hair done. He opened the door and immediately started laughing and I rolled my eyes and walked into his house. I really just wanted to walk away but I decided to see what was going on. I was going to try with Bruce if he was willing. He had a two-story home with two bedrooms. It was okay and very lovely, but it was built for a man. He had a pool table in the dining room instead of a table. Yes, he was a bachelor with a girlfriend. "What is so funny Bruce?" I asked as I sat at his marble countertop. "Your hair is ugly," he responded in a nasty tone. Most men did not care about a hairstyle if they liked a woman. He was doing too much. "Well I like it Bruce so that discussion is over." I said and ate a piece of candy that was in my purse. He twisted his face up with disgust. I was confused I didn't know what was Bruce's problem. "Ugh how big do you want to get?" He asked and I felt self-conscious. Although we were the only people in the room, I was still embarrassed. I was comfortable with my weight, my hips, and my ass. Still his words stung no matter how comfortable you are with yourself if someone else disapproves of your looks it will make you feel self-doubt. "As big as I want, why are you going to leave me or something?" I questioned with an attitude. Suddenly he leaned down and kissed my lips, that made me feel better. That is until he opened his mouth. "No, we have too many businesses together baby." I was taken aback. Well damn did he really feel that way about me? I had never seen this side of Bruce, his true colors was starting to show. "Oh so that is how you feel about me?" I wanted to know. Bruce sighed, "I feel things about you Niya a lot of things about you." I looked at Bruce

I needed to look in his eyes. He avoided eye contact with me. I did not know what he was thinking, and I did not know what he meant when he said that. This was not about some hairstyle he couldn't be treating me this way over a hairstyle. "So, in a couple of years will you be ready to settle down and marry me?" I asked hell I needed to know before I got to deep. At first, he was all about me and the kids but for real even before the Atlanta trip he was acting weird. We had only been dating for about seven months, but we had known each other now for almost two years. He was pursuing me really hard but now it seemed like he got what he wanted and was no longer interested. "Settle down come on Niya we never talked about that before. I am not ready for that type of commitment." "So why are we building an empire together if we not going to be together?" I asked. Susan had warned me about men like him. She told me she had gone to school with these men and they were looking for their next come up. Whatever woman could help build them socially and financially in the business world they were looking to use them. The same thing Lawrence was doing to Chiquita. "Come on honey let's not get into this." "Okay Bruce whatever you say." I stood up and stormed out of his house. I did not know why he had changed but I was going to change too. Forget Bruce he was using me to get where he needed to be. I was starting to think that he did not have any other businesses. He never talked about them and I think the income I supplied was the only income he had. I was going to tell him about the business deal with the salon and how Susan said that I would make a lot of money, but I was going to keep that to myself. I had been avoiding Bruce for a week. I just did not know what he really wanted from me. He had sent me a bouquet of roses and told me he was sorry, but I did not know why he was sorry. Was it because he was messing things up with me in a business way or was, he sorry because he was messing things up with me with our relationship. I had thanked him for the roses, and he had come over and we had sex but that was it. The sex was like a thank you for the roses type of thing I could tell that things were changing for the worse between us. I really did like Bruce we looked good together but so did Hakeem and I and look how that relationship ended. It was time to go back to Atlanta and finalize everything with Rashad. Cedes was going to stay and watch the kids again while we went to look around the club because we wanted to fix it up and change it a bit. This was Rashad's project, so we let him strategize. He had put up most of the money so the little we added was just enough to get a percentage but he felt like we were a part of the business too, so I guess he wanted to bounce some ideas off us for the weekend. I was glad I had a Nanny to help with the kids because once again I had to leave my kids. Rashad came and got us from the airport and was looking super sexy with a red Polo shirt and some tan pants. I know one thing he was fine as usual. He saw my red hair and the response I got from him was the one I should have gotten from Bruce. "Damn girl," he said, "you look good." He said right in front of Bruce I could tell Bruce was mad but he did not say anything. Rashad turned to Bruce. "No offense bro but your lady look good I know you been knocking that out ever since she got the new look. What made you change your hair?" "I never had a different style before, so I thought it was time for something different. Thanks." I said and my panties started dripping because I started thinking about the way he had eaten my love box before. "It is nice." He complimented me. I smiled at him. Rashad was so damn fine. As we got into his truck Bruce and Rashad talked business as I sat thinking about ways, I could fuck Rashad. Bruce and I were still not on good terms and to be honest I was okay with that. I did not call him, he called me, and I focused on my business. When I we got to Rashad's house, I noticed that something was missing. Well not something but someone. "Where is Italy?" I asked. "She on business she will be back later this week." He said. I was glad that Italy was gone I liked her, but I knew she wanted Rashad. With her not around maybe I could have some alone time with Rashad. That was wishful thinking because Bruce was here too. We ordered some Chinese food and watched movies. Rashad was telling us about how he wanted to change the club and we were bouncing ideas off each others head while Bruce sat there like he was bored. Bruce had money but he did not have the creativity to be a businessman. That was the reason he wanted me to help him build his "empire" because he lacked motivation. He was a good boss, but I kept the books, I paid the bills, I did the ordering, the scheduling, the pay rate, the expansions, everything I did it all he did was drive around a check on the different sites and make sure things were getting done. That was an important part of the business, but he still was not doing as much as could have been doing. After sitting there and thinking about it the truth was right in my face. Bruce didn't have any other companies he was eating off me. I should have known but I was a fool. He had talked a good game to me, and it was my own fault. Rashad made us a glass of wine and as we sat sipping and talking Bruce seemed to be getting sleepy. I do not know why the hell he had not done anything all week. Before I knew it, he was passed out on the couch. It was strange the way that Bruce had passed out. Rashad got and poked him. "Good he finally out, damn he was getting on my nerves." He said and turned to me. I immediately got afraid and put the glass down. This man was crazy did he just drug Bruce? "Don' t be scared Niya I didn't put anything in your drink. I always do this to Bruce when he comes down to visit. He gets on my nerves I just drug him and put him to bed. He wakes up and thinks he was drinking too much." I started laughing. We grabbed our glasses and clinked. I laughed again, "Damn man you don't like Bruce, do you?" "No, I really don't I just know he had the extra money to put on this business. He has said some racist shit over the years, and I do not appreciate it. I have known him all my life and all my life he has treated me like I was not shit because my mother is black. He acts as if we are not brothers. Him, Rick, and Tyler have always cast me out and jumped on me when we were younger. It wasn't until I was about fourteen and my older brother Darien taught me how to box that I came to Wisconsin and they thought they were going to jump on me. I beat the shit out of all three of them." Wow I had not known this. "Our father told me I did not have to visit anymore. He wanted his children to be close, but he could see that that was not going to work." Rashad needed to get this off his chest and I was ready to listen. "Bruce's mother Chelsea was not upset about the breakup she treated me good. She loved me and I think that pissed Bruce off even more. Our sister Elise she doesn't even fuck with Bruce because she is married to a black man Bruce talks so much bullshit about Elise for no reason." I nodded my head at Rashad. "He has mentioned Elise, but he never really talks about her. How many siblings do your guys have?" "Rick is the eldest brother. Then it is Tyler and I we are the same age, but he is older. Our mothers were pregnant at the same time. Then it is Rebecca, then Bruce, Elise is the baby. Rebecca lives in Chicago." "Yes, I know we expanded our business out there she runs one of our cleaning offices." "Yeah I know Rebecca is a pure sweetheart you should go out and meet her one day. She could tell you a lot. She could tell you much more than I know. Our brother Tyler he a fag who dresses in women's clothes." I started laughing. Bruce had not shared all this information with me. Hell, I was starting to wonder if I needed to build an "empire" with his brother. We sat and talked for hours and I really did like Rashad. He told me about his brother Darien who was in jail and would be getting out soon. He even explained the Italy situation. Darien was using Italy to run drugs back and forth. I don't know where, but he was making money in jail. Then he told me the shocking truth about himself, he was a drug dealer. He told me that he wanted to do more though and that is why he wanted to invest in this strip club. I admired his drive to change. "So, I gotta ask you Niya? How did you like my oral performance?" His question took me by surprise. Although I was shock my kitty was happy. I was tipsy and she wanted some more. I grabbed his hand. "Shit I want some more." He led me upstairs and we left Bruce downstairs slumped over on the couch. Rashad was about to eat me like a box of chocolate and this time I could scream as loud as I wanted. It was good and he left me shaking, shivering, and wanting more after that. He denied me access and told me that we were not going to have sex. I cuddled next to him satisfied and we drifted off to sleep. All I could smell was Rashad's cologne and it was breathtaking. I loved the way this man was holding me the entire night. I did not know how I was going to leave him when it was time to go but I know one thing I needed to know more about Bruce. That night I did not have a nightmare about Hakeem and I fighting. I did not think about Hakeem and all the beatings he had given me. I did not dream about me killing Hakeem and me going to jail no I was having a peaceful dream of flowers and doves. Then there was a loud banging that interrupted my peaceful sleep. I looked up to see Rashad staring at me. "Hey Rashad! Do you know where Niya is at?" Bruce was yelling through the door. I looked around and realized I was cuddled in my boyfriend's bed. Damn we were caught what was going to do. I jumped up I was in a panic. "Hold on a second bro!" He yelled back at Bruce. He grabbed my hand and pulled me into his master bathroom. He whispered, "shut up I am going to get him out the house for breakfast you stay in here until we leave. Get dressed and say you went on a walk when we come back." "Okay," I whispered back. Rashad closed his bathroom door and I sat in the bathtub and listened. I don't know why I was so scared I did not want Bruce to find me in here. "Bro why the hell you banging like the police?" Rashad asked opening the door. "Do you know where Niya at?" I could tell he was in the bedroom. Oh man I hope he didn't want to come in the bathroom. "She said she was going for a walk. You got pretty fucked up last night man and you was talking shit to her again." Rashad lied. I had to giggle. Rashad was funny and was lying so good to Bruce. It sounded like Bruce sat on the bed because I heard a squeak. "Man fuck her she has a damn mouth on her and then she has that ugly ass red hair in her head. Ugh she look like a hoodrat." I could not believe what I was hearing but sure enough I was hearing it with my own ears. "I do not know she looked good to me," Rashad said playfully but I knew he was serious. Fuck you Bruce I know somebody who like it and it happens to be your fine ass brother, I thought to myself. "Well you fuck her then," Bruce laughed. "As soon as I figure out how to get her to sign off on all the businesses, I am dumping her ass." My heart stopped. What did he mean by that? "What you mean?" Rashad's tone was serious. "I just want the businesses to myself and leave her ass broke. I am not going to pay for shit. I am going to keep her ass sprung off this good dick and then I will have her stupid ass sign off the businesses to me." Bruce stated confidently. "Damn bro that is why you been fucking with her? You one cold muthafucka." Rashad said. "I mean I like her but fuck a bitch it's all about the cash. Shit if I didn't like her my dick wouldn't get hard. Shit I knew when I met her that she was an easy target. It took a while, but all good things will come to those who wait you know what I'm saying." Oh, so I was just cash and a cum partner. I had something for that muthafucka! Well, I had to think of a plan. He was not going to take my businesses from me. "Damn," Rashad said sounding sad, "you want to go get something to eat?" he asked. "Yea sure" I heard Bruce get up from the bed "I have a slight hangover." I heard Rashad opening his closet getting his clothes out. "So, you don't mind if I get at Niya?" He chuckled but I knew he was serious. "Man, she not going to talk to you but as soon as I am done with the stupid bitch, I will pass you those digits." Bruce chuckled. That was all I needed to hear. That muthafucka did not give two fucks about me so you know what all the love I had for him was gone. Here I was contemplating being with him and here he was with a damn plan to leave me broke. He knew I had kids to provide for and that did not even matter. All that mattered to him was his greed and quest for power. I was glad for this ease dropping moment. Yes, my heart ached a bit, but my head hurt the most. I was thinking fast and hard because I needed to devise a plan to get him out the contracts and leave him flat on his ass.

BRUCE

Rashad wanted to play stupid like I didn't know he had fucked Niya. I know he fucked her the first time we came to Atlanta. I only wanted to take over her businesses but now the bitch was really garbage to me. I should have beat his ass. At first, I was pissed but when that bitch came over my house with that red ass hair in her head, I knew she was not on my level and it was time to give her up. Yup Rashad could have the hood rat. As soon as we walked in the Waffle House the aroma hit me it smelled so damn good. I wanted to eat everything. Every time I came to Rashad's house, I drank the wine and it got me fucked up. He had some type of wine that was stronger than damn alcohol. The shit made me hungr y and thirsty every morning. I was eating my waffles when I got a text from Italy. Rashad I never really talked when we went out it was just something to do. I looked down and she had sent me a picture of her perky titties. Yeah, she wanted me to fuck her while I was in town, but I didn't think that was going to happen. I ignored her and decided to text Teresa a 'GM' text yeah, she loved that shit. I know she was a bit pissed at me because she said that it was taking too long to trick Niya and that she was tired of hearing about Niya. I was mad because I felt like she was up to no good too. She was being un grateful, and I was doing all this shit for her. That's bitches for you ungra teful. "You talk to Rebeccca lately?" Rashad surprisingly asked me. I shook my head no and kept eating. "That's a fucking lie!" He yelled "I know she is running your office in Chicago." Damn it Niya must have told him last night when I was out cold. "So, fucking what?" I wasn't no punk. "I find it funny since she haven't told me, so she is hiding something and so are you. So, let me just say this it bet not be no funny business." "I asked Becca not to tell you because it wasn't for you and Darien to know." "Yeah well Becca never hides anything from me or Darien." He said matter of factly. "Well maybe Darien knew, and you was the one left out of the scenario." I encouraged. I knew why Becca hadn't told Rashad that she was helping me she didn't want to feel weak. Darien didn't know shit about it I just threw that in since he wanted to be fucking my damn girlfriend. "Bullshit Darien would have told me. So, the bullshit y'all trying to pull is not acceptable I will be telling Dad about this." "Fuck Dad!" I yelled. He made me lose my appetite I was ready to go. I headed out to the car. This trip needed to be over.

Chapter Eight
ANIYA

——————◦◦⟫⟩◦◦⟨⟨◦◦——————

When Rashad and Bruce got back from breakfast I had showered and was dressed. It was scandalize the way that Bruce had talked down on me and the way he was trying to deceive me was pure bullshit. Here I was being a good girlfriend and business partner and he was trying to scheme on me the entire time. True enough I had allowed his brother to perform oral sex on me twice but still I was a good girlfriend at least I had not just totally broken it off with him. Bruce walked up to me and gave me a kiss and I gave him one back. Rashad looked at me to make sure I was okay because he knew I had heard everything, and Bruce knew nothing. I looked in his eyes to let him know I was not fucked up about it. At the end of the day this was my excuse to get out of the relationship. Hell, Rashad was my type of guy I liked him and after last night I knew he liked me. If it was not for those business contracts, I would have dropped Bruce then and there. I had to be smart about the situation I could not believe I did not know he was up to no good. The first time I met with Bruce I was distraught, and the death of Hakeem was fresh. I had to devise a plan Bruce was not going to take my businesses. We met up with Mr. Richards and his nephew Crenshaw. We exchanged money and the strip club was officially ours. Even Crenshaw couldn't keep his eyes off of me when he saw my hair. He complimented me and Bruce laughed like it was funny, and I rolled my eyes and thanked Crenshaw. Bruce was full of hate. We looked around the strip club I was pleased to see that they made some minor upgrades. "Are you going to be able to run everything?" I asked Rashad. "Hell, yeah I been waiting and wanting to go legit for a long while now," he smiled. I smiled at Rashad he had potential to be a great businessman. We left the strip club and we went to the house I needed to take a nap. Our trip was going to be short because I wanted to get back to my kids. After I woke up, I prepared for the flight back home. It was dark as I made my way down the stairs.

Rashad was sitting in the kitchen eating a burger. "You ready to leave me shawty?" He flirted. I looked around and didn't see Bruce. "Not really," I flirted back. "Put my number in your phone," Rashad demanded. I pulled out my phone and put his number in my phone. "You see what he had to say about you shawty, you need to leave him and get with me for real." There he had laid everything out on the table. What was I going to do? I did not know. But I would think about it and figure something out. I was ready to get on with my life I thought Bruce would be the perfect man, but I was wrong. I think it had a great deal to do with the fact that Bruce was white I thought a white man would be different, but I was finding out that men are men, dogs are dogs, I had to start choosing wisely and right now I did not know if Rashad was the man for me either. They were brothers and not only that all these men in my life had shown that they were one person in the beginning and then they changed on me. I ignored Bruce the entire plane ride. All he wanted to talk about was how he hated Rashad and was happy to be getting a piece of the pie, but he was mad because he had to do it with him. He kept talking about how he was going to allow Rashad to run the club but after a couple of months he was taking over. He had his nerves how can he think that he could take that man business when he did not even put in twenty percent of the money. Rashad had put up most of the money we had just put up the extra cost to fix the place up. After I had talked Mr. Richards down Rashad really did not need us to buy the club, but he did need for us to help do the upgrades. Bruce didn't see that he was such a selfish person and I was seeing it firsthand. When we made it to Wisconsin Bruce drove me home, he wanted to know if I wanted him to come over, I declined. He had me fucked up and he did not even know why. He had laughed and insulted me our entire trip. Not only that but after hearing how he really felt about me I was just too done. I walked in my house and was surprised that it was not loud. No one was in the living room but that was to be expected it was the middle of the night. I went upstairs and looked in on Malcolm and Deena and they were sleep. Jon-Jon, Chris, and Junior were on Malcolm's floor asleep. I went in my room and Cedes was in my bed in her bra and panties asleep. I was tired myself. I stripped down to my panties and bra and got in the bed with her. The bed squeaked a bit and I guess that woke her up or she was not sleep all the way "Hey girl I didn't hear you come in," she said. "I was trying to be quiet it is so late." I said looking at Cedes. Cedes was gorgeous even though her hair was a bit messed up. I wanted to know why she stayed with Vanessa. She was a beautiful girl on the outside, but she was lost on the inside. "Why are you still with Vanessa and still dealing with Lawrence?" I asked her I wanted to know. We were sitting in the bed staring at each other. "I don't know, I been thinking about that too and I think it has to do with me not loving myself." I was astonished. Cedes didn't love herself. Please she was a perfect size eight and she was fucking beautiful. "Girl you are gorgeous," I complimented her. "You think so?" She asked me as if she was a child getting verification from her parents. "Hell yeah!" "If you think I am so beautiful then why you never took heed to my advances?" I was confused. "What do you mean?" She moved close and kissed my lips. At first, I was going to stop her but Cedes smelled so good. I could not resist. My pussy was getting wet with every kiss and I was allowing her to explore my body. She moved from my mouth to my neck and it felt good. The way she moved her tongue around my neck had me soaking wet. She pulled my titties out of my bra and started licking my nipples. I was in pure bliss. "Cedes I can't do this," I blurted out. She stopped licking, "you not doing anything I am." Cedes connected her soft lips to my nipples and I melted. She went down to my love box and I wanted to tell her to stop but I wanted to know if she was any good. As she licked all my secret spots I exploded with orgasm after orgasm. I lay with her that night and I was ashamed that I had let her seduce me. I had never been with a woman and I did not know why I had allowed Cedes to perform oral sex on me. I did not know what was happening to me first it was Rashad and now it was Cedes I hope she did not think that I wanted a relationship with her. The head was good, but I could not see myself with a woman. That night I know that Cedes had enjoyed seducing me, but I had never been with a woman. I was perplexed too much was going on at once. First, I find out my boyfriend does not like me, then I let his brother perform oral sex on me, and now I allow my kid's siblings mother perform oral sex on me. Plus, she is also my assistant/nanny. My life was getting more complex by the day. Cedes had fallen asleep but I was still awake. I decided to go and lay in my office I did not want her to think that we were going to be in a relationship. The next morning was weird. We got the kids ready for school and did not say much I told Cedes she could have the day off. It was due to the fact that I was too ashamed to face her. I did not know what I was going to do. I think she was getting the vibe that I was not ready to be with a woman. She had not said much when she woke up the next morning, she knew that I had left her in the bed alone and I think that sort of hurt her. I wanted to explain things more to her, but I did not know the words to say. I soaked in the bath and Bruce texted me. He was acting like he was so in love with me asking me how was my day going? I was lying telling him I was so busy. Yeah, I was busy, busy ignoring his ass. I could not believe he was pretending to care. Well he had pretended all these mq+onths why stop now. I had even allowed him around my children and that right there was a no, no. I had to push the Cedes situation out of my head right now and figure out how to deal with Bruce. I shot Rashad a text and waited for a response, but he did not send one. Maybe he was busy so I would just have to wait for a response. I was not about to cook so I ordered pizza for me and the kids and decided to stay in the house too much was going on, and I did not know what was about to happen, but I did have a bad feeling. As I lay in bed that night, I could not help but think about Bruce, Cedes, and Rashad. What was happening to me? I was always a one woman, man even when I was having sex with my mother's boyfriend by force, I was still only having sex with one person. I needed to get myself together. I know I wanted to be done with Bruce and I know I was not at all trying to be with Cedes. But Rashad

I was just getting to know him, and I really did like him but the fact that he had not texted me back had me baffled. I fell asleep with my mind pacing and thinking a mile a minute. The next couple of days I was highly pissed. Cedes had been calling in and I did not know why. Ever since I had hired her, she was always at my house and she never called in. I did need time to think but I also needed help. I was not about to let a little oral sex get in the way of my business and how it ran. Thankfully Chiquita was able to pick the kids up because I had to go to the salon and pick up my percentage of the money that was being made. The salon was doing well. I had paid Sheila the back rent, money of five thousand dollars and now I was getting a percentage of "Lovely Ladies" I was too damn happy. All I did was stack my money. I spent when necessary, but I also saved my kids would not struggle in life I knew that is what Hakeem was working hard for to provide his kids a nice life lifestyle. I had not spent any time with my best friend Mya, so I decided to invite her over to keep me company. I needed to catch up with her anyway. She came over and her long curly hair was beautiful as usual. Even though she did not know my past history she was always there for me. When I w hffas homeless and broke, she allowed the kids and I to stay at her family's hotel free of charge and they fed us. That was a real friend and when I got that insurance money from Hakeem's death, I hit her hand. Mya did not have to work she was spoiled rotten, but she did have a receptionist job at a nursing home. She had a boyfriend Chris, but he got some other woman pregnant and left her. Mya could not have kids and it broke her heart that he had left her. She was dating another man Donald, so I wanted to see how that was going. I was always busy but when I needed Mya she was always there. "So how are you and Donald?" I asked as I sipped on the frappe that she bought me from McDonalds. "Fuck Donald he is married." She rolled her eyes. "No! What?" I was in shock they had been dating for about four months he seemed like a nice gentleman a little old but nice. "Yes, his old ass is married. I was going through his phone one day and saw the number that said wife. So, I memorized the number and called. Girl she picks up I say how do you know Donald? She likes I am his wife. I say his legal wife? She says yes, we been married for twenty years. I was so mad." She looked mad too all the things that Chris put her through only for her to find another man who put her through more bullshit. "So how are you and Bruce" she asked changing the subject. "Fuck Bruce," she looked surprised. I knew Mya for years and I was always a private person. She knew about all the good things in my life. When I dated Hakeem, I never allowed her to see me when I was bruised up. She didn't know about how James raped me either. I didn't want the judgment, but right now I really needed someone to talk to about Bruce. "Girl when we were in Atlanta, I overheard him talking shit about me to his brother. He really does not like me and is really trying to get me to sign over my businesses to him without him paying for them." I said in one breath and it was good to finally let words out. I had to come to the realization that Bruce had used me. "Damn that's cold do you think he had been plotting this from the beginning?" I nodded my head. "Hell yeah." My boyfriend was a conniving little snake I was pissed just thinking about it. As I sat and thought about his nasty ways and listened to Mya talk about Donald some more, I got a text from Rashad. Rashad 'Sorry sweetheart I been busy with the club but I been thinking about you.' His text made me smile. There was potential in Rashad. As Mya babbled on and on, I got lost in my thoughts. Bruce was not going to hold me back and he was not going to take what was rightfully mine. I was going to have to show him what kind of bitch I could be, it definitely wasn't a stupid bitch.

CEDES

I was so fucking confused. I did not know why the hell I had performed oral sex on Niya last night, but I knew I could not face her. I called in the next day and told her that I was sick after about three days Nessa started to look at me funny. She came in from her job with working with the youth. I was watching television sitting in my pajamas. The boys were at their after school, activities. Nessa looked at me sitting there eating a tube of vanilla ice cream. "Damn what's going on baby you ain't been going to work?"

I shook my head no and continued to watch television. She looked at me again and came closer. Before I knew what was happening, she punched me in my nose. I thought my nose was broken as I grabbed it. "What the fuck!" I yelled. "Bitch you fucking Niya?" She screamed at me. My eyes told on me as they got wider. Before I knew it her foot was flying towards my face. She kicked me on the side of my head. "Ouch!" I screamed out. "Bitch you a nasty ass hoe!" She quickly grabbed my hair and drug me to the floor. "Stop Nessa!" I screamed. I had a sew in and it hurt for her to be pulling my hair. She dragged me a couple feet across the floor. Nessa stopped pulling me and started kicking me in my stomach. "Oh you want me to stop you nasty bitch! You a sick bitch! Fucking hoe!" Her kicks was hurting me because she still had on her boots, I didn't know what to do. I screamed out in pain and settled into the fetal position until she was finished. She finally let me up after about two minutes. I went to the bathroom and cleaned myself up. I was crying so bad that my body was shaking. I looked at the time and the boys were going to be home pretty soon. I covered my face up like I always did and prepared dinner. Nessa didn't say shit to me. The boys ate and we had our time laying on the couch watching television. I stayed in the living room while Nessa was in the room. Once the boys were asleep, I tiptoed to grab my coat and head to the hotel. I knew Lawrence was there waiting for me. It was cold that night, so I put a pep in my step as I hurried into the hotel's lobby. I rode the elevator up to the fourth floor. I knocked on the door and Lawrence's fine ass was waiting for me. He kissed my lips as I walked into the room. I had not combed my hair or anything I just came as is. "Damn did Nessa beat your ass again?" He asked the question like he was asking me how my day was. Damn how many times had he seen me like this. I started crying. "I can't do this anymore Lawrence." I cried. "What you mean you can't do what anymore?" "I know you want me to leave Nessa, but I can't I love her. I have to move on from this situation." He looked shocked. "Oh, so you choosing her over me? You dumb as fuck! Get the fuck out!" He screamed and threw the glass against the wall. I had never seen him so mad. "Just please try to understand," he cut me off. "Bitch get the fuck out before I beat your ass!" I was surprised but I hauled ass because I know I could not take another ass whooping. I went home and got in bed next to Nessa. She wasn't sleep though she was lying there. "I see you snuck out to see your bitch" she scared the shit out of me when she spoke. "I didn't." I tried to explain but just like Lawrence she cut me off. "You know what? This ain't me Cedes I shouldn't be putting my hands on you and I don't want to. It would be best if you just left. So, pack you and your kids shit up and be gone by the time I get home from work tomorrow." I didn't even know what to say I was hurt. I had just left Lawrence for her and she was turning her back on me. I was crying. I couldn't lay in the bed next to her. I went and got in my car. I opened my glove compartment box and took my gun out. I been had this gun just for protection, no one even knew I had it not even Nessa. I took the gun out and contemplated on shooting my brains out. I wasn't the one hurting me though Nessa was. She was the one who saved me from her abusive brother. Now here she was doing me the same way. I wanted Nessa she was all I knew she was the only person my kids knew. I couldn't go back to Aniya she showed me that she didn't want me. Nessa was not just going to leave me she knew I didn't have anyone. As I made my way back into the house it was dark. I opened the bedroom door and I could hear Nessa snoring. I closed the door behind me. That bitch was sleeping good after she just kicked me out. She didn't give a fuck about no one but herself. I raised the gun up and pointed at her sleeping head. The tears rolled down my eyes, it was all a blur as I pulled the trigger. BLAT! Her brains splattered across the wall. I smiled that bitch wasn't going to leave me now and I was not going to leave her. I heard Junior come knock on the door. "Mama you okay?" He asked. "Yeah boy just go lay back down." I made sure the door was locked and got in the bed with Nessa she was my love and I wasn't going anywhere. She loved me and I loved her. I know I had fucked up but so what this shit was forever.

Chapter Nine
ANIYA

ya and I had decided to go out on the town. I needed to treat my friend because she was going through some things just like I was. We needed this time together and it was going to take my mind off all the bullshit that Bruce was putting me through. Chiquita agreed to watch the kids and I was grateful for that. I had not talked to Cedes since the night that she performed oral sex on me. She texted to say she was sick but that was days ago. I think that maybe Vanessa was beating on her again. I was not sure but that is what I really thought was going on. Mya had started helping with the companies, so I was grateful. I had spoken to Bruce and he was pissed at me. I was dodging him and treating him like the business partner he was. He had been asking me to come over I had declined and when he found out I was going out he was furious. He had texted me while I was getting dressed, I texted him back that I was going out and he called me. "Where are you going?" He asked as soon as I picked up. "Downtown with Mya" I said sounding irritated as I put my lipstick on. "So, you can go hang out with your friends and not your man?" I wanted to laugh he was not my man and as soon as I figured out how to get out of these contracts with him, he would not be my business partner either. "She is going through some shit right now Bruce. So, look I have to see about her she always was there for me so stop your damn crying." I said he was pissing me off just the fakeness in his voice was enough to make me go insane. He did not even reply back he just hung up in my face Mya and I laughed fuck him. I dressed in some white booty shorts with a red top that hung low at the chest part. I was looking good. Mya had even decided to get slutty she was smaller than me, so she had on a dress that had the openings in the side. We were taking shots of Patron before we went to party. Mya and I had never went out because neither one of us were the going out type. But since I was single, and she was single it was time to mingle. I was tipsy before we left the house, so

Mya drove my Porsche to the bar downtown. Mya could hold her liquor better than I could. I needed air to get my buzz down. It was packed when we got inside, and it was good because we needed to enjoy ourselves. We started dancing and surprisingly Mya knew how to dance I mean she was really dancing. I was surprised I had known her since middle school, and I had not once seen her dance. Well I was dealing with so many problems at home with James and then I met Hakeem and had kids I really did not have time to hang out. I was happy that I was finally living my life. We were having the time of our lives. The men loved us. Two bad redbones hell who would not love us, we were getting free drinks and I would dance with the guys and she would dance with the guys and they would all buy us drinks. There was this one guy who was steady watching Mya and I told her she should try him out. Mya had always dated white men for some reason. She was mixed with black and white, but I always seen her with white men. The guy who was watching her was black and fine. He was dark skinned with a low haircut. He was not that tall, but he was about her height with her heels on. When he smiled though he had the prettiest white teeth I had ever seen. I would have jumped all over that man, but I had enough problems and also it seemed like he was checking for Mya. "Girl dude is looking at you." I said she rolled her eyes. "I know he been looking at me all night, he not my type." I laughed. What did she mean by that? "So fine is not your type?" I asked hell he was fine as hell. "Yeah he is fine, but he is just so dark." She answered. "What you mean girl fine is fine no matter what color." I said and gave her an evil eye. She looked at me and she smiled. She was cute, but she needed to keep an open mind, "Mya sometimes you have to take a chance on things that you never took a chance on before. You have to think outside of the box." "You right I am going to go talk to him. Gotta think out the box right" she said and sashayed over to him. Damn right you have to think out the box. I know I was thinking out the box. I had a boyfriend who really was not my boyfriend and I was halfway sleeping with his brother and I was sleeping with my Nanny/Personal assistant I was on a roll. I was doing things that I had never dreamed of doing. I knew it was not right, but things were happening so fast I just did not know how to stop things. I must admit I liked the romantic love affairs just a little bit. I decided to text Rashad. Me 'what you doing?' I got back to dancing and I was also watching and making sure pretty smile was not on no bullshit with my girl. I felt my phone vibrate and I checked it and it was Rashad. Rashad 'thinking about your sexy ass.' That put a smile on my face. I made my way to the bar so that I could sit and think of a reply. I sipped on my Patron as I messaged him back. Me 'oh really so when do you want to see me?' I was so much into my phone that I did not notice the guys around me. Most importantly I was did not notice Bruce walking into the bar with another chick. My phone vibrated with a message from Mya. Mya 'look to your left and you will see Bruce in here with some white blonde hair chick.' I spun my head so quickly to see him that I got dizzy. Sure, enough there was Bruce up on here with some bitch. I finished off my drink and strutted my way over to him and the chick. They were sitting in a booth. Bruce looked up and saw me and smiled. I do not know if he was trying to play it off or if he was happy that I had caught him. "What the fuck is this Bruce?" I yelled but it really wasn't a yell because the music was loud. "A friend!" He responded back. I glared at him. The music was making my head hurt. "Come outside!" I yelled at him and he followed. He better fucking had. We made it to the patio and at this point I was angry. "Oh, so that is the type of shit you want to do we can have friends and shit now?" I questioned. I knew he did not want me, and I did not want him, but we had not broken up yet. "Baby calm down. Yes, we can have friends I never said we could not. Who you here with?" He asked looking around. "Mya my friend Mya," I said I was slurring my words, but I was standing straight. I was a bit dizzy and I was glad that I was accustomed to wearing heels because if I had not been, I would have fell on my ass. "Okay well go find her and do not worry about me. Can you do that?" He replied in a nasty tone. "So, you want us to be done Bruce?" "No, but you been acting funny, so I do not know what you want." He was right. I was the one who was acting funny. He had asked me several times to go out with him or to come over and I would make up an excuse every time. I had not forgotten those harsh words he said to his brother in Atlanta, but I really did need to stay on his good side so that I could get his name off the contracts. "I am so sorry baby," I pleaded I was drunk, but my mind was not gone I needed to get back on Bruce's good side. "I have been going through so much Cedes have been calling in and I have been doing all the work on my own. I know I should have told you, but I just did not want you to worry." He looked at me. "Damn why didn't you say this before I thought that red hair was getting to your brains." He just had to mention the red hair. "Baby you have to communicate these things with me so I can know to help you. I can get someone hired by Monday to come over and help you." "No baby Mya said she will help so I figured it out." He grabbed me around my waist and kissed me. He made my pussy wet and I wanted more maybe it was the alcohol, but I wanted Bruce right now. But his playmate came and interrupted everything. "What the hell is this Bruce?" She yelled. We stopped kissing and turned to look at her. Damn she was pretty he damn sure knew how to pick them. She was supermodel thin with blue eyes. She was wearing the hell out of that lingerie type dress. She was definitely a beauty. "I am his woman that's what the hell this is!" I yelled. Mya and her dark-skinned friend had come out now and Mya was right at my side. I did not know if Mya was a fighter, but I was happy she was here even though I could handle it myself. "What?" she looked at Bruce, "you did not say you had a girlfriend." "Well you did not ask either." He had gotten caught up, but he did not seem to care. The girl just looked at him and walked off. I started laughing this shit had to be a joke. I would have whooped her ass if I had really been into Bruce, but he was nothing to me. "What the fuck was she talking about Bruce?" I asked but I knew he was not going to answer. "Go home and I will be there in a minute okay." That was his reply to me. I did not feel like arguing so Mya

123

and I left. Her friend who was named Tre walked us to the car. They chatted the entire time we walked, and I was trying to sober myself up. We got in the car and Mya drove me home. I told her to take my car and to just bring it back in the morning. She gave me a hug and let me know everything was going to be okay. I think she thought that I was so quiet because I had just seen Bruce cheating on me, but the truth was, I was really drunk. I stripped down to my panties and went to lie in my bed. I put my phone on the charger and saw that I had an unanswered text. It was from Rashad he had replied back. Rashad 'ASAP.' I smiled that could definitely be arranged. Bruce did not even call or come by that night I knew he had made the decision to chase after that Barbie looking bitch and that was fine. I was okay with it. I was planning on getting out of the contracts with him and making him look stupid. After I thought about tonight events, I knew Bruce had set it up he wanted me to see him with that chick hell I had told him where I was going. I did not know what games he was trying to play but it was time for me to do a little digging around. Before I did that, I needed to plan a trip to Atlanta alone without the company of Bruce. I missed my baby Rashad and I wanted to see if what I was feeling was a mutual thing.

BRUCE

Once I made sure that Aniya was gone, I went to go check on Teresa shewas pissed but she played her part. I had to make sure my baby was good. She lived in a big ass house. It was four bedrooms and three bathrooms. I pulled up behind her Ferrari. I used my key. Her house smelled like chocolate chip cookies. She was sitting at her vanity looking at herself in the mirror. "Baby I am so sorry about that." I started to explain. She turned around and had tears in her eyes. I did not understand I mean shit she knew about Aniya. "Bruce she is beautiful I can't compete with her." I was appalled I could not believe Teresa thought that Aniya was beautiful she was cute, but she had nothing on my Teresa. I ran to her and fell to my knees. "You are gorgeous my Teresa! No one is better than you! I only need you!" I screamed at her so that she knew I was serious. "Really Bruce?" "Yes, babe you have to believe no one compares to you." I kissed her. She tasted like mint. I reached inside her silk robe and she didn't have any panties. "You ready for Daddy?" "Of course," she smiled. I picked her up and carried her to the bed. I could never do that with Aniya she was too big. Teresa was just right for me. I opened her legs and gave her this dick. We made love all night. I know I had told Niya that I was coming to check on her but fuck her, Teresa was first priority. I laid next to my future wife and I swore I smelled a male's scent, but I must have been mistaken she only had eyes for me.

Chapter Ten
ANIYA

It was the middle of the week when I had planned my trip to see Rashad. I still had not heard from Cedes. She had stopped texting me and every time I went to call her it went to the voicemail. Something was not right and after I got back from my trip, I was going to see what exactly was going on. I had asked Chiquita and she said she had not heard from Vanessa. They were not close anyways so that was not a surprise. I had officially hired Mya as my personal assistant/ nanny, so the kids were at her house. I told her all about Rashad and I thought she was going to judge me but amazingly she didn't. She actually encouraged it since I had told her the horrible things Bruce had said about me. That made me feels good because I had hid plenty of things from her that now I wish I had told her. Maybe things for the kids and I would have been different. I was so afraid of judgment that I did not tell her, but I had known Mya since we were teenagers and she had always been a good friend to me. I touched down in Atlanta and I was so happy to see Rashad. As soon as I had touched down my phone started ringing it was Bruce. I had not spoken to him since the incident at the bar but now was not the time. I pressed ignore and headed towards Rashad. He was looking grade A of course. He got a hotel not too far from the airport for us to enjoy. Italy was back and we wanted to be alone and we needed our privacy. Rashad got us a nice little hotel room I was going to stay until the next night and then head home. Rashad was a pure gentleman. He pampered me just like a woman should be pampered. He made us a bubble bath and we got in together. I had gotten in the tub with Hakeem before, but it was all because he had beaten me. He would get in the tub sometimes to comfort me but never on some romantic shit. This time it was, and we connected as we talked about the things that had transpired. "You should not even worry because he do not like her. He is evil he is using her like he trying to use you."

He said and even though I did not want Bruce I still did not want him to want someone else. When we got out of the tub Rashad took his time and dried my body from head to toe. He wrapped my body back with the towel and rubbed lotion all over me. It felt so good and I loved the way he touched and massaged my body. He was a real romantic guy and he knew just how to make a woman feel special. I wanted Rashad so bad but to my surprise we did not have sex that night. I wanted to and I know he wanted to, but I laid in his arms and he talked to me. Rashad told me everything about his dreams and the things he desired in life. I was so excited to actually have this feeling again. Hakeem would do this with me and tell me how he felt and what he wanted for our future. I loved Hakeem and I wanted us to have a future. Tears started falling from my eyes and Rashad was confused. I always did this, I always thought of Hakeem. "What is wrong did I say anything wrong?" "No, you just making me think about my first love." "Your first love oh so where is he now?" He asked. "He is dead." I said as tears rolled down my cheek. I had not cried in a long time about Hakeem, but I did miss him dearly. I was strong on the outside and I lied to myself on the inside, but the truth was I was hurting, and I wanted to be loved again. I believed Hakeem loved me even if he didn't know how to show it. Men can go through things that women will never know about and take it out on us. But they hurt just the same as we do. They get hurt and have feelings just as we do. I just wish I could have helped Hakeem battle his demons. I was not strong enough emotionally to help him I see that now. I was selfish I took my true love and now I was stuck raising our kids by ourselves. "It's alright baby girl I am here now." I looked up at Rashad. "Do you mean that? Or are you just saying something right now?" I asked and I really wanted to know where I stood with this man. "For real girl I liked you when I saw you. You are beautiful with a fat ass and you smart as hell." He said and I smiled that was all true. "So is your first love is that your baby daddy?" I shook my head yes. "See right there your baby daddy is gone so you don't have any baby daddy problems and you have your own money. You are any real man's dream girl and I am a real man." He said and I believed him. That night we did not make love we fell in love by opening up to each other. Sometimes you can fall in love with a person's words and not even know but I know I was falling for Rashad. Just how he wanted me I also wanted him. The next morning, we got dressed and went out to breakfast at the Waffle House. We don't have Waffle House in Wisconsin, so the food was something different and delicious. I loved the city and I loved spending time with Rashad. He took me to the Atlanta Zoo, and we saw the animals that was a different type of date, but I could see he was spontaneous. It was a wonderful experience and I was happy that he was here with me and that I had stopped being scared and pursued him. I know I was wrong for being here with Rashad while Bruce was steady calling me. The truth was Bruce did not give a fuck about me he only cared about himself. He was using me, and I did not see why I was a good person and I was definitely good to him. It was time for me to go back home and Rashad and I had not had sex yet. I tried to but he stopped me. "Look Niya I get pussy all the time I am not going to lie to you. I want you to get shit straighten out so that you can be just mine. I know you still sleeping with my brother and I can't get mad. First get that situation solved so you can be all mine." He said and I understood no man wanted his woman to technically belong to someone else. As we rode to the airport, I wanted to ask Rashad a question that had been on my mind a lot lately. "Rashad do you think that Bruce is racist?" I asked and he started laughing what the hell was he laughing for? "No baby he not a racist he is a pure asshole. He don't just hate black people he hate white people too. You should really talk to my sister Rebecca she will give you an idea of what you are dealing with." He gave me her number. "Why you just can't tell me?" I asked. "Because I am not about to tell her business it is for her to tell." He said and that was that. He gave me a long kiss good-bye before I boarded my plane and I did not want to leave but I had to get back to my house and kids. When I made it home the kids were already in bed. I thanked Mya and she left and went home. She told me she would be back at about ten the next day. That was fine because I know she needed some extra rest. I had not heard from Cedes but I know I needed to deal with her and see what was up with her. We had become rather close and now she was acting so distant. I was going to stop by there and see what was going on as soon as Mya made it in the morning. I woke Malcolm up first in the morning he was always the hardest to wake up. He went to go brush his teeth and wash his face. I went to wake my baby girl Deena up and she looked so peaceful in her sleep she was gorgeous. When she got up, she smiled and said, "Mommy I saw daddy." "Where at honey where did you see your daddy?" "In my sleep he was holding me and rocking me he told me he loved us." She said sitting in my lap. "Oh, really did you tell him you loved him back?" "I sure did, and I asked him why he did not want to be my Daddy anymore." She said and it broke my heart. "He do want to be your daddy and he will always be your daddy honey he just had to go to heaven." "Yeah that is what he said, and he said he feel good and that he is watching us even you Mama." That sent chills over my body I did not want the man I killed to be watching over me. "Really that is good how about you go brush your teeth and wash your face like your brother." Deena had spooked me a bit saying that her father was watching over us. I knew he was watching over us. I could feel it in my sleep it felt like his eyes were watching me as I slept. It was scary sometimes and calming at other times. I got dressed after the kids left and headed on my journey to see what Cedes had been up to. I had tried to call her phone, but it went to the voicemail. I even tried to call the boys phone and their phones were going straight to the voicemail. I did not know what I was about to get into, but I know the whole drive to her and Vanessa's apartment my stomach was in knots. I had a horrible feeling and I felt scared for some odd reason.

RASHAD

Aniya was the one! I know she was fucking my brother, but she is the fucking one. I gave her Rebecca's number so that it would make it easier for her to leave that sick son of a bitch. I decided to call my mother and tell her that I had found the one. I know Aniya would be the one to help me to get back in the game and she would be a real rider. "OG what's good?" I screamed into the phone. "Boy why the hell you so happy?" "Cause Mama Aniya is the one." "What you mean the one for what?" "The one for me Mama." There was a pause. "Now ain't she dating Bruce? You know that girl kind of slow right if she dating that boy." "I know Mama she ain't that smart but she going to be perfect for me." "Whatever let me run this by your daddy first." "Well I already gave her Rebecca's number, so the shit is motion." "Why the fuck would you do that!" She yelled into the phone. "Because she needs to know!" I yelled back into the phone and she hung up the phone in my face. I couldn't wait for Darien to call me he was going to be on my side. We all knew that once Aniya found out the devil that Bruce was, she would not want to fuck with him. She needed to know so that shit would be easier for her to choose me. It was like she knew he was using her, but she was holding some type of faith that he wasn't. Bruce would fuck over his own Mama to get more money for Teresa and Teresa's ass didn't even want him. He was stupid and blind to the fact that Teresa was using him to fatten her back account. I didn't give a damn though I needed that extra money to buy the strip club from Mr. Richards so that he could build a trust level with me. I had done that, so I no longer needed Bruce.

Chapter Eleven
ANIYA

When I pulled up, I did not see her car, so I tried her phone again. This time it rang but I still did not get an answer. I decided to go up and see what was going on. Vanessa and Cedes stayed on the second floor of an eight-family apartment on the Southside. I really did not want to climb the steps. I rang the bell, but no one answered. I rang the lady downstairs bell and she buzzed me in. She was a young black woman with two kids. I liked her she always spoke when I saw her. She was in the hall when I came in the building. "Girl you came to check on Cedes?" She asked and her short hair was barely fitting into the ponytail I really needed to refer her to "Lovely Ladies" but right now I was on a mission. I had seen her about three times before, but I was glad she remembered who I was. "Yeah she not answering I don't know if she mad at me or what." "Well between you and me if I had not seen her then I would have thought she was dead. She and Vanessa been fighting a lot and it is something serious." She whispered. When she said that my heart dropped, I ran up the stairs and she went back in her house. I was glad that she was a nosey neighbor, but she should have called the police if she thought something was wrong. I banged on the door "Cedes! Vanessa! One of yall open up!" I did not hear anything. I tried the door, but it was locked. "Cedes! Boys! Junior! Chris! Are you guys in there it is Niya!" I yelled and I heard movement. "Open up boys! What is going on?" Junior cracked the door open and pulled me in. My nose got whiff of a stench. "What is going on? Where is your mother?" I asked. "She gone she went to get something to eat." He said in a calm tone. "Okay where is Vanessa?" I asked and he gave me a weird look and said nothing, so I tried another question "Where are your brothers?" "They in their rooms" I walked to the back and the smell got worse and all the doors were closed. I checked on the boys and they were happy to see me. They came and hugged me. "You came to get us?" Jon-Jon asked. "Yeah but I need to know where is Vanessa?" I asked again. "She in the room," he said and Junior shot him a look. It was something going on here. The boys were barely talking, and it was a bad odor coming from somewhere. I knew something was wrong because Cedes was a clean woman she did not like to be in filth. And that smell was like something was dying somewhere. "I am going to go check." I said. And Junior tried to stop me. "No you should just go." He told me. "Junior go sit down." I knew something was going on and I rushed to the first room where I knew Cedes and Vanessa slept. When I opened the door, it was the most horrible thing I had ever seen. As soon as I opened the door the smell hit me. It was a mixture of death and blood that was the smell. Vanessa was on the right side of the bed covered in blood. The wall was covered with blood and so was the floor. She looked horrific it was like half of her face was off and I could see her brains and some of her brains were splattered on the wall and I started screaming, "Oh my God! Oh my God! What happened!" I was screaming and I did not hear Cedes come in the house. "Who the fuck let you in?" It was Cedes's voice, but it was cold like I had never heard before. I turned around and it was Cedes like I had never seen her before. Her hair was parted down the middle and was in a neat ponytail. She did look like herself, but her eyes were cold no life were left in them. "Junior let me in" I said in a low voice. She looked pissed. "What is going on here?" I asked even though I already knew it was obvious that Cedes had killed Vanessa. "Bitch you see what the fuck is going on I killed that bitch," she said, and she slammed the door. I looked down and saw that she had a gun. I backed up as she raised it to my head. "Cedes girl what are you doing?" I said and I had to admit I was scared. She had me in a hard place and I did not know what to do. I was still doing my kickboxing, but I had never been in a position where a gun was pointed at my head. "Stop asking me stupid fucking questions." She said, "I really do like you Niya and that is why I haven't been answering my phone, but you just have to be nosey don't you?" She asked and cocked the pistol back. This bitch was going to kill me I had to think fast she had lost her mind I had to bring her back down to Earth because right now I knew she was on Pluto. "I thought you were ignoring me because you didn't want to be with me." I said trying to buy time because she was coming closer to me. "What do you mean?" She asked and I could tell I had her listening. I saw a little twinkle in her eyes, and I knew that she really did like me. Well I don't think she really liked me I think she really wanted to be loved. "I thought we had a connection and then you just disappeared." I said and the more I talked the closer she got to me with the gun. This bitch had flipped her lid I needed to think fast. I think I had her defenses down a bit. "I know all the shit that you went through and I just thought that I could comfort you." She looked me in my eyes, and I could tell she was going for the bullshit I was saying. "I had no idea that you were this stressed out why didn't you tell me?" I had broken her she began to talk and explain and at the same time she had put the gun down by her waist. I kicked the gun out of her hand, and it stunned her as the gun went across the room. I did not give her time to react I kicked her in the mouth. She fell and I punched her in her mouth. Just then I heard the door bust open and it was the cops. "Let her go!" They demanded. I immediately got up and put my hands in the air. I did not know who called the police, but I know one thing that I needed to get out of this situation fast. They arrested both of us and we were hauled off to jail. I was pissed I was trying to be a good friend and almost got killed and now I was locked up. I called Mya when I was getting booked and told her to call Susan, Bruce, Rashad, and Chiquita. I felt bad for Chiquita at that moment because I had realized she had lost her brother and sister. They took me into the interrogation room and started asking me questions. I told them how everything happened, but it seemed as if Cedes was in the other room telling lies. She had told them that I had shot her girlfriend and she had started fighting me and that is when they came in. Her story would have been a good case had her sons not called the police Junior was the one who called the police when he saw that I was in danger and Jon-Jon and Chris backed up my story. Thanks to those guys I was released, and Mya came to get me. After sitting in the jail for three hours I was happy to be let out. It reminded me of when they interrogated me after Hakeem's death. They had me in a similar room and I was scared. They said that they had noticed that maybe Hakeem did have an asthma attack, but it seem like it could have been prevented. They kept asking me why I had not called the police and I stuck with my story that I had went to hide in the bathroom and I did not know that he was having an asthma attack. I told them I was scared for my life and that he had been beating me and I was hiding it for years. I explained to them that he was beating me in front of my children, but they did not care. They held me for twenty- four hours and let me go but they told me they would be back after the autopsy. I guess the autopsy report told them the story because they did not come back to pick me up. I was grateful then and I was grateful now. I had walked into a fucked-up situation and I did not know what had exactly happened, but I was glad that I was not going to jail. No one was there to take the boys, so I allowed them to stay with me. I was happy they had helped me out. If it was not for them, I would probably still be in jail. They could had lied and told the police that I was the one who had killed Vanessa, but they didn't. Cedes was their mother and I know they loved her, but I was happy that they knew right from wrong. I was appreciative I did not know what was about to happen to Cedes but I knew one thing that was some bullshit that she tried to put me in, and I did not appreciate it. Susan was on top of everything she was not a criminal lawyer, but she knew people. I needed to see what was going to be going on with the kids. It had been a week since they had released me, and the boys were staying with me. I had not heard anything from Bruce, but Rashad had been checking on me and making sure everything was okay. He made a few calls to a private investigator and found out that Cedes's mother was still alive. I called her mother and was surprised when she was willing to take the boys. I allowed the boys to finish out the week with me and I was going to take them to Waukesha, WI that was the city that their Grandmother was in. It was an hour away. It was Friday after school and I packed their things up and we rented a van and went on our trip. The summer was going to be starting in a week anyway so the transfer of school would not be bad. They were brilliant kids, so they were on top of their work. I had still not heard anything from Bruce. I knew he was okay because our workers said that they had seen him. I knew what he was doing he was trying to figure out how to turn this event around on me to make me look bad and take over the businesses. I stopped trying to reach out to him and just went on with my plans to do what I needed to do for the kids. Bruce would not ever win this game he was playing with me. We made it to Cedes's mother's house late around nine o'clock that night. Mya had come with me just because I did not know this woman, I wanted to be sure to have someone here to help if I needed to get the kids away. I did not know what was possible after all the crazy events that had transpired. Cedes's mother was beautiful just like her. Cedes's mother was thin and looked really good for her age. She was darker than Cedes but her skin was gorgeous just the same. She invited us in, and her home was beautiful. She had five bedrooms and three-bathroom, home it was lovely. She said she stayed alone. Cedes's mother had two older children who were boys and they were both in jail too. Her eldest son Marvin was in jail for a double homicide and her other son Martin was there for a rape and murder of a woman. I felt sorry for the lady because she did not have anyone left. I know that is why she wanted to take in her grandchildren they were all she had left. I was curious to know why Cedes's mother had not wanted her when she found out she was pregnant. "I never turned my back on Mercedes she turned her back on me. Martin my son had just got convicted of the rape and murder of Cedes's friend Kim. I do not know what happened, but my son is in jail for life both of them my other son Marvin went to jail a couple of years ago for a double homicide." Damn I felt sorry for her she was alone. "I had told Mercedes she could stay here but she did not want too. I think she had something to hide that she was running away from. I let her go and live her life. I never saw any of my grandchildren until today. She never called or reached out. She knew I would have helped her." She started crying, "it is so sad to know my children are all locked away like animals, but you know what is even sadder is that the children that I raised are killers." I hugged her and thought that it was sad she had lost all of her children and not only that she had to live with what her children had done. "They were cold hearted anyway. It is because of their father he was a killer and that is why they are killers like that it is in their DNA." I would have never known that about Cedes she was such a sweet girl. "Mercedes was sweet very sweet, but it was just a matter of time before she turned into a killer like their father, he is in prison too. He was a notorious serial killer. I had not known until the day the police had come to pick him up. I was heartbroken. He had left me with $75,000 and that is how I built my business. The day that he left us was the day I became a strong, single mother, who was about her money " Cedes mother was inspiring I loved talking to her. She was one tough lady who made a bad decision and turned her life around. I knew if she could do it then I damn sure could do it too. Before we left, I needed to have a private conversation with Bertha. She seemed to really know her shit and that was good. I had Susan who was legally smart, but I needed someone like Bertha who was street smart. I knew that the boys were going to be in good hands. I just hope that they were not going to grow up and do anything to get locked up. Bertha looked so happy to have them that I knew her broken heart was mended or damn near there. I knocked on her bedroom door and she told me to come in. It was time for us to leave but I needed her help. I sat down on her bed and watched her comb her graying shoulder length hair. "What is bothering you honey?" She turned and looked at me. I knew it was obvious and Bertha had that motherly intuition. "I have this contract with my so-called business partner who is also my so-called boyfriend that I am trying to get out of. He has a percentage of all my businesses and I just do not know how to get him to sign over all my businesses to me without me giving him some type of money." She looked at me and she seemed defeated also. "Damn I have to really think on that situation honey I have never done anything so stupid." She laughed and I did a little chuckle. It was stupid to let Bruce get a percentage of my business. He had not called me ever since I had Mya call him and tell him I was locked up. He knew I was out, but he did not stop to see if I was okay or anything. I knew he did not care by the conversation I overheard but now he was making it very obvious he did not care. Rashad had been there he had helped me find Bertha. "Listen baby give me some time to think about this situation you are in and I will surely get back to you. I know my way around things, and I want to think long and hard on how to get you out of this situation so don't give up. Keep being his so-called girlfriend while I come up with a plan." I hugged her and thanked her. I knew that Bertha would come up with something to help me out of this situation. I really wanted to be done with Bruce and move on and I definitely did not want him to get any more of my money. "I really appreciate you," I told her. "Do you have some background information on him that could maybe help you with this?" She asked. "No not really I am kind of in love with his brother and he told me about their past history but nothing to deep that could be damaging. I know his brother keep telling me to call Rebecca." I said. "Now who is Rebecca?" She asked. "Rebecca is their little sister she also runs a business for us in Chicago." "She just might be the key to what you need. Reach out to her and find out as much information you can on this guy. I can tell you are too trustworthy of people Niya." She was dead on, "you see how you trusted my daughter and how she tried to betray you. The reason why Cedes did not bother you and Hakeem was because she was not sure that Junior was Hakeem's baby. Cedes is a manipulator girl. I can look at you and tell that you have a good heart, but I can also look at you and tell that you are ruthless, you are a thinker. Use that to your advantage stop being so afraid of your dark side use that in a good line of attack and everything will work out for you now this guy who you may be in love with what is his name?" "Rashad." "Okay so this is your boyfriend's brother you need to get as much information as possible about both of them. They may be scheming on you together." She was right I had never thought about that. "Talk to the sister Rebecca I believe that she will give you the answers you really need. Not just about your boyfriend but about Rashad also. I think that you need to really get it together and see what is going on in your world. You have two children who are counting on you. You told me about how Hakeem was an abuser do not let his death be in vain." I looked at her strange I did not get what she was trying to say. She caught on to my confused look and explained "You went through a horrible time with Hakeem and you defeated those demons even if it was by default. Now you have this hurdle that you did not see coming. Hakeem was a major point in your life and yes, he beat you, but he also took care of you and left and those babies something to build on. Do not let some no good, man come snatch you success away." She was right I needed to fight for my businesses that my baby daddy had worked hard to get for our children and me. I left Bertha's house with a new understanding of things. She was right I did need to figure things out and Rebecca may be the person to help me. I was too trustworthy. Rashad had texted me to check on me, but I ignored him. I needed to regain focus on my life. These men were deterring me from what I really needed and set out to do and that was become a successful businesswoman. I needed to get back on my shit and get out of these contracts. It was time for me to find out who Bruce really was and who Rashad really was. I wanted to drop Bruce and maybe pick up Rashad, but I needed to be sure. I liked Rashad I really did, and it was going to be hard for me to ignore him, but I had too many things going on right now. I also needed to talk to Cedes to see what the hell was going on and what had happened with her and Vanessa I wished her the best, but the bitch was out of line for putting me in that shit. I also needed to check on Chiquita and make sure she was good. Damn! Chiquita! She was first priority right now. She had been a bitch to me when Hakeem had died but we had made up. She had been great to me ever since. Not only had she lost her biological mother and father she had also lost Deena and Malcolm the couple who had taken her in after she had ran away. She had been abused and mistreated. She did not have any parents and no friends she had a conniving ass fiancee. She had her brother and sister and now they were gone. I wanted to see her to make sure she was okay to let her know that I was here for her. That would be my first stop before I headed out to Chicago.

Chapter Twelve
ANIYA

———⊷∘⊳⟫⊰⊕⊱⟪⊲∘⊷———

Mya was so helpful she agreed to watch the kids I must admit she was a great friend. She had to cancel her date with Tre, and I was felt bad, but I had wanted to talk to Chiquita. She sounded sad over the phone and I just wanted to see how she was really doing. I knew that she was taking Vanessa's death hard and once again she would be putting one of her family members in the ground. It was a typical cold day in Wisconsin where there was much breeze and little sun. For it to be close to summer it sure felt like winter. I made it over to the apartment where Hakeem and I had once lived. Chiquita had taken it from me and left me and my kids homeless. That was in the past though we had gotten past that, and I was here to console a friend. I knew that it was difficult for her to accept Hakeem's death because they were close. I really did not know how she was taking Vanessa's death. I felt like she never really cared for Vanessa because she didn't endure the same abuse that her and Hakeem had. One thing is for sure Vanessa was dealing with something I just didn't know what. I made my way up the stairs to the door that I once occupied with Hakeem and my kids. I still had the key, so I let myself into the main door. I was afraid that Chiquita would turn me away because she might not have wanted me to be there for her. She was such a strong woman that she sometimes dealt with things alone. I walked up to the wooden door and I heard some talking it sounded as if Chiquita was arguing with someone. I could only hear Chiquita's voice and no one else. I was assuming she was on the phone I was going to interrupt her and knock on the door when I heard my phone vibrate. I had turned my phone on vibrate when I got out the car so we would not be interrupted I looked down at my phone and saw that I had a text from Mya. Mya 'I hope you haven't made it to Chiquita's house yet. If so then get up and leave right now. Make up a lie. Get back now. My heart started racing I did not know what was going on. There was silence on the other door I quickly turned around and ran down the stairs. I was hoping like hell she did not see me. Mya had to just learn something, and it had to be important. The entire ride to the house my mind was racing. What was it that Mya needed to tell me? I had told her about the abuse that Chiquita and Hakeem had suffered. Mya was my friend and she was on my side. I wish I would have opened up to her sooner. She told me that she didn't give a fuck what abuse he suffered that did not give him the right to hit you. She said if anything that should have made him love you more. She was right and wrong at the same time. You would have thought he would have wanted to love me more but instead it made him want me to suffer like he had. When I pulled up to my house everything looked good. The only strange thing was there was a black SUV in the front of my house. I quickly got out of the car because I did not know if my kids were safe. I stormed inside the house and was surprised to see Tre sitting in my living room with Mya. "Sit down," Mya said to me and I sat on my black chair right across from the black loveseat they were sitting on. "What's up?" I asked looking at Tre. I know he was Mya's new friend, but I didn't know him. "Tell your kids to go in their room or somewhere private so that we can talk" Tre said. He did not say it in a threatening way, but I still had my guard up. I told Malcolm to take his sister to their playroom and I would be in there to see about them. I told Malcolm a long time ago that if I felt like we were in danger that I would tell him to go in the playroom and I would check on them. That was the signal to let him know to lock the door and wait for me. Malcolm looked at me and grabbed his sister's hand. He knew what to do. He was a strong little fella. As they disappeared up the stairs, I looked at Tre, I needed answers. "Okay I know you are wondering what is going on. So, when Mya cancelled our date I called her and we were talking. I was asking her some questions about your friend Chiquita. I am not trying to get in your business but how do you know Chiquita?" Tre asked. "Oh, that is my baby daddy's sister." I said I wanted to know where he was going with this, I relaxed a bit because he was just asking about Chiquita. "Your baby daddy is Hakeem?" "Yes," I wanted to know how he knew this. I was feeling very funny. "Okay Mya told me about Vanessa being murdered and I do not know if she told you that I am a private investigator for the police. Well I have been trying to uncover the death of Malcolm and A'Deena the man and woman that took Chiquita and Hakeem in." "What do you mean you are investigating their deaths?" I was so confused now that I did not know what to do. "Look Malcolm and A'Deena took them in and helped them and they were healthy people, but they became very ill. They both died and the police have reason to believe that Chiquita and Hakeem killed them. It was a closed case since it is so old but A'Deena's and Malcolm's family members want answers. Their cousin hired me to investigate." I damn near hit the floor. I did not know all of this. Chiquita never mentioned any of this to me. Hell, why would she and why did Hakeem make me name our children after them. "What?" I whispered. "Well let me correct that we do not think that Hakeem had anything to do with the death just Chiquita. And now we have reason to believe that she was involved in Vanessa's death." He said and I could barely breath I did not know why this was being said. "Why do you guys think that?" I asked. "She is the beneficiary on Vanessa's insurance policy just like she was on Malcolm's and A' Deena's insurance policy. Not only was that but her fiancé Lawrence cheating with Vanessa's long time, partner Mercedes and Chiquita knew about it." This was too much for me to swallow so Chiquita knew about the affair. Damn I wanted to ask her what was going on. "We know that Vanessa was killed by Mercedes, but we think that there is more to the story than what meets the eye. I just want you to be careful around her because she is dangerous." "Do you know that she also have insurance policies in your children's name?" I shook my head no. What the hell was she up to? "It seems as if she had Hakeem do it and he has never changed it over I think that you need to get your paperwork together. Chiquita is up to no good. We have been trying to connect her to A'Deena's and Malcolm's death for a while now. Hell, it was before I became a private investigator. A'Deena and Malcolm were very important in the community and they were loved." I didn't know what to say to Tre this was so much to take in. One thing for sure I wasn't going to let Malcolm and Deena go over her house. I was scared to be alone and I asked Mya to stay with me and the kids. There was no telling if Chiquita would kill me to get to my kids. Mya and Tre both stayed with me and that made me feel good. My kids got in the bed with me and I decided to text Rashad. I was scared and I needed some comfort and I knew that Bruce was not going to give it to me. Once I texted Rashad, he called me right away he had not heard from me in a while I guess he was really worried. That made me feel special although I did not know where I stood with him. I was just happy to be wanted with no strings attached right now. "Damn girl how you been?"

He questioned. I started to cry I told him everything I had learned about Chiquita. I was so scared for my kids that I did not know what to do. I felt like I was being watched. Tre said that he did not think that Chiquita was plotting anything against me, but I was still afraid. "You need to move here with me so that I could protect you guys" Rashad said. "Are you serious?" I asked. I needed some certainty that he was serious because I did not need any more let downs. "Hell, yeah it is too much going on and plus hell you are a good friend of mine." That crushed me when he said that. He only wanted to be my friend? "But you need to do is really get out of those contracts with Bruce you need to break free from all bullshit for real. I can tell you are a good woman and I just do not like you and those kids going through so much." That was a nice thing to say but he only thought of me as a friend and honestly, I did not fully trust him I think he could sense that too. "Did you ever reach out to my sister Rebecca?" He asked. I had not forgotten about Rebecca but there were so many things going on that I had not even called her. "No not yet." "Okay do that she will tell you all you need to know about me and Bruce." It was like he put emphasis on me to let me know that he knew that I did not trust him. "Have you talked to Bruce?" "Nope he has not called since I got locked up. I have been calling him, but he has not returned any of my phone calls." I did not understand that before I got arrested, we were on pretty good terms. I knew he did not want to be with me, and he was probably tired of pretending. That was okay but he still could pretend to be a good friend to me since we were in these deals together. I had a feeling that Bruce was plotting and planning on me and I was five steps behind him. I needed to get ahead of him, but I had so much going on right now that I could not even think straight. "Fuck him you just need to do what you have to do to get all of your money. If you find out how to get him out your contracts, then you let me know because I will definitely get him out of the contract with the strip club." He laughed. I did not know why he was laughing because shit Bruce was kind of getting over on both of us. Not only that but Bruce almost blew the strip club deal hell maybe Rashad knew something that I did not know. I knew one thing I was going to find out what he knew though. I needed to know everything I could. I was in a bad predicament with Chiquita and it was required that I get to know what Bruce was capable of and up to. It seemed like Rashad knew something, but he was adamant on not telling me. "Trust me I will. I am going to go to bed I am drained from all the bullshit I found out today." I was really tired I needed to get my kids away from Chiquita. I needed to think of a way to get out of these contracts my head was hurting from all the things that I was going through and I really needed to get things under control. "Okay goodnight sweetheart." Rashad said to me. We hung up the phone and he sent me a kissy face. I smiled and cuddled next to my children. I was going to figure all this shit out sooner than later and first thing in the morning I was going to call Rebecca. I had a feeling that Rebecca would tell me something's that I did not want to know but what I needed to know. In the pit of my stomach I knew that Bruce had things going on that no one could imagine not even me and that is why I needed to get the answers.

RASHAD

As soon as I hung up the phone from Aniya I went back to my room. I had a brown skinned honey named Caramel fucking with me tonight. She worked for me at the club. She was fine as hell, but she was a hoe, so I was going to hit it and quit fucking with her as soon as tomorrow. She was laying in my bed naked and her 34B were perky I could see her erect nipples. I walked over to her and pulled my dick out of my boxers. There was no words needed to be exchanged. I picked up the condom from the dresser and made my way over to the bed. I was imagining she was Aniya. I didn't know what it was about Aniya, but I wanted to make her mines. All the hoes I done fucked didn't mean shit because I wanted her to be my wife. "Open your legs" I commanded Caramel after I put the condom on. She did as she was told. Her shaven pussy didn't even look good. This was going to be my first time fucking her. She had been giving me head at the strip club, but I was not trying to fuck on her. She had finally gotten me to bring her home. Well not her but my main bitch at the time Keisha was acting up and I did not feel like kissing her ass to get no pussy. As soon as I stuck my dick in her I couldn't even feel shit. She was moaning and I was wondering what the fuck was going on. I tried to pump a bit faster, but the shit was not working. Her pussy was wack as fuck. After five minutes of trying to keep my dick hard my shit went limp, I pulled out and got off Caramel. "You came already?" She asked. I didn't even respond back. I guess she thought she had done something because she had the nerve to ask me some dumb shit. "So, Shad can you get my hair done?" I turned and looked at the bitch like she was crazy. "What nigga you just got some pussy so now you can't pay a bitch?" I slapped her in her face "Get your damn clothes on bitch! You weak pussy ass bitch you ain't worth me buying you a $15 weave!" She jumped out of the bed and all I could smell was ass. "Ugh bitch and your pussy stank! Get your ass the fuck out!" She started putting on her clothes "how am I going to get home?" I threw the bitch forty dollars "Get the fuck out!" She scurried out of my house. I got my ass in the shower damn that bitch wasn't even worth it, and her pussy was stinking. Yeah, I was going to fire her ass tomorrow because her hygiene was not on point. Those thirsty ass niggas maybe liked to smell fish, but I didn't do seafood. As soon as I turned off the water, I heard my phone ringing again. I wrapped my white towel around my body and went to answer my phone. I saw that it was my Pops, good my Moms was getting on my damn nerves calling to talk for him. "What up Pops?" I laid down on my bed it was cold in my house. I pulled my blanket over my body. "Hey boy I am upset with you." He stated. "That's not a surprise." I said I already knew what he was talking about. He started to explaining that doing business with Mr. Richards was not going to be a good idea. I knew the nigga was under investigation, so my best bet was to be low. After he kept saying how I needed to find another connect and that I was stupid he finally said the magic words. "But you are my son, so I am in." He sighed. My smile got real big "thanks Pops and stop worrying." "You a damn fool boy." He said before he hung up. This was great news my father was going to help me start this shit back up yes, I was going to be a kingpin and I was going to have a fly ass chick on my arm, Aniya.

Chapter Thirteen

ANIYA

—◦◦≫≫⊕◦⊕◦⊕◦≪≪◦◦—

A s soon as I called Rebecca, I was happy. That nervous feeling, I felt before totally went away as soon as I heard her voice. She was very inviting and that made me relax. I was drinking some orange juice in the kitchen while Mya and Tre watched television with Malcolm and A'Deena. I actually trusted Tre and that was different for me because I rarely trusted anybody, and everyone could see why. With all the things that had went on a person could understand that I was very untrustworthy. "Hello is this Rebecca?" I questioned sounding unsure of myself. "Yes, this is her who is calling?" She sounded so cheerful like she was having the best day of her life. "Niya" I paused "Niya I am Bruce's girlfriend." I said I did not know what else to say. I had never talked to her before. Bruce had expanded the business, so I never had a reason to talk to Rebecca. "So, you finally got the courage to call me thank God. How soon can we meet?" She got right to the point. She was waiting on my call Rashad must have told her about me. We set up a time to meet each other and I asked her if it was okay that I bring Mya, Tre, and the kids with me. She said she did not care if that made me feels better than I could bring twenty people. I laughed I was happy that she was such a nice person. I know I needed some answers and I was happy that she was going to give them to me. School was over for the kids and we were set to hit the road that Thursday. Tre was going to drive us in his SUV so that we did not have to get a rental. I had talked to Chiquita and kept it cool so that she was not suspicious, but she wanted to get the kids and I told her that I was taking them on a trip. I did not know what I was going to do or what excuse I was going to make up to avoid her getting the kids because sooner or later she would notice that I was acting funny. She told me that she was going to have a private funeral for Vanessa, and I told her that I would come to pay my respects. I knew that was not going to happen, but I just said to make it sound good. If I did, I wanted Tre to come with me though to make sure she was not up to anything. I don't know ever since I had found out about Chiquita, I started to be afraid. Although Tre did not say that she was after me or wanted to harm me I was still afraid that she was up to something. I had even talked to Bruce he took me on a date to the movies. He had begged and pleaded with me saying that he was sorry that he was not there for me in my time of need, but he was just so confused. I knew it was some bullshit, but I acted as if I had missed him so much. I even had sex with him, and I tell you when you are trying to prove a point to someone it is like the sex gets better. I had never experienced sex with Bruce like that. I do not know if me being mad at him made the sex better or if it was because he had not seen me and that made the sex better. I know one thing he pissed me off once we got done. I was getting off of him and once I laid next to him, he had the nerve to say. "That was good girl damn I am so happy that you took that red out. The blonde looks way better on you." Seriously like what was it about my hair that he did not like. I had changed my hair into a curly blonde weave that was similar to Beyonce weave yes, I looked good with blonde or red so why was he criticizing. "So is that the reason you have been avoiding me" I asked but I knew the real reason. Susan had a friend that was a lawyer who worked for Bruce his name was Sampson. Sampson had told Susan that Bruce was doing the paperwork that would have me sign over my rights to the businesses. Sampson had agreed to talk to me and I was happy that Sampson was on my side. "No babe I was just scared when you got locked up. I did not want it to jeopardize our businesses." That was a lie he was trying to use that shit against me. I knew his game and I was ready to play it little did he know. Even Sampson told me just like Bertha that I needed to get more information on Bruce and our plan would be perfect I was ready to get this cockroach. Even though Sampson had been Bruce's lawyer he did not even like him. Sampson was an old school brother who was a smooth talker. He stood 5' 7 and he had smooth brown skin. He was older but his hair was not gray I knew that he probably dyed his hair. I had met him once before with Bruce and the way he looked at me when we walked in to his office was hilarious. Bruce introduced me as his lady and Sampson eyebrows went up and he said, "I did not know anybody liked you." We all laughed. At this time Bruce and I were not official, but he was trying hard. He wanted me to meet with Sampson so that I could feel comfortable with the Chicago expansion. I had already talked to Susan about the expansion and she thought that it was a good idea, but she said that I should not do it with Bruce. She asked me, "why are you putting this man on all of your businesses?" I looked at her and to be honest I really did not have a good answer. Hell, he was telling me to do it and I was doing it. At this time, I really did not have feelings for Bruce, but I did trust him as a friend. That was worth more than us being in a relationship we were friends. "He is okay," I told her. "I advise you not to put his name on all the business." She said. I rolled my eyes and said with an attitude "I just wanted to know if I should expand, I do not need a lecture." Apparently, I did not know anything because now I had put his name on all my shit, and he was trying to take my companies away from me. I should have known that if his lawyer was surprised anybody liked him that I should have dug deeper. I thought it was a joke though, but Sampson was serious he knew what kind of asshole Bruce was and here I was stuck in this situation with him. As we headed to Chicago my stomach was in knots. Bruce was calling me, but I was ignoring his calls. Fuck him two could play that game and at this point and time I was starting to think that speaking to Rebecca was the perfect thing to do. I wanted to know everything. I wish I had gotten background information on Hakeem before I had to lay him to rest then things may have been different, I might not had to kill him. I pushed him out of my head the deed was done, and truth be told if I had to do it again if I had to kill Bruce then I would. I was not going to stop at any limits to protect my money and my children's future. I was hoping that it did not come to that, but I was game for anything at this point. Rashad had been calling me and he told me to make sure I get all I needed from Rebecca I did not know what that meant but I was glad he was on my side. It was crazy to me that Bruce was his brother, but he was helping me. I had lost my trust in people and that is why I needed Tre and Mya to come with me I wanted to make sure nothing I heard was fake and that nothing I heard was mistaken for something else. I needed witnesses for what I heard. I needed a support team and right now they were all I had. Going through life without a support team can be brutal I knew that firsthand. I had gone through all the bullshit with my Mom and James by myself and when I found Hakeem, he was my support system, but he used that against me. I know he love me, but he could not love me right because he did not love himself. I had Mya by my side the entire time and she had not changed on me. I looked at that and started to appreciate her more and more each day. I knew I could trust her. I felt like I could trust Tre also he came off as a real honest guy. I was kind of mad that he was interested in Mya because truth be told if she had not been a really good friend, I would have definitely tried his chocolate ass. But I would never do that to her. I had never been to Chicago to visit and I was enjoying the view of the city. I called Rebecca and she gave me the exact directions and I still did not know what she was talking about but thankfully we had GPS. I was shocked when we pulled up to Rebecca's house. I have to tell you the woman was living lovely. She had a gate at the front of her mansion. I called to tell her we were outside, and she opened the gates. It was like I was in heaven I thought this could not be possible. I did not understand I know that two thousand a month she was getting from running the cleaning company was not supporting her. She met us at the door, and I have to admit Rebecca was stunning. Her sun-tanned skin was beautiful, and she had about a dozen freckles across her face. Her green emerald eyes were beautiful and that red hair of hers was gorgeous. That hourglass figure was to die for I loved the way she looked and when she saw me, she hugged me. "I am so glad you came." She said and she smelled wonderful like she laid in a bed of flowers. She invited us into her beautiful home. She had all types of sweet treats for the kids and she guided us into the living room. Mya stayed with the children and Tre and I went into Rebecca's family room to talk. She opened a glass of wine and poured herself a glass. She did not even allow me to ask any questions she just started to talk about Bruce as if she had waited a million years to tell someone. "Bruce was always a sick child. And when I say sick, I do not mean ill. He would always do things to torture us as children. Tyler, Rick, Bruce and I were the oldest children Elise came after us. Larry is her father although Bruce always tries to act as if we all have the same father." She walked over to a picture and grabbed it up off the table. "This is Elise gorgeous, isn't she?" Rebecca asked. "Yes, she is." I agreed. Elise was gorgeous. She looked similar to Rebecca, but she had blonde hair, but the eyes and the freckles were the same. Her figure was not an hourglass, but she was still gorgeous "My baby sister I love her so any ways. Rashad that is my other brother he is such a sweetheart and whenever he came to town we hung out. No one else liked Rashad the other brothers would jump on him. Mama would scream for them to get off of him, but Bruce had Tyler and Rick trained and they were the older brothers. Bruce was always an evil guy as he got older, I guess he camouflaged himself better, but Bruce will always be Bruce." She started laughing and sat on the white couch. "What?" I was confused as to why she was laughing. "Do you know that Rashad drugs Bruce when he comes to town?" I laughed too. "Girl he is something else but as we got older Bruce started to cling onto Rashad more once Rashad had pulled away from us. I had started spending the summer in Atlanta with Rashad, Darien, their mother and my father. Their mother was wonderful but so was my mother and I could see how my father was torn in between those two lovely women." "Do you have a picture of your mother?" I cut her off. I wanted to see their mother I had seen Rashad's mother now I wanted to see Bruce's mother. She got up and went to where her pictures were stacked. She handed me a picture of their mother and some black guy. "That is mother and father." She said and I damn near lost my mind, so their father was black, but Bruce looks white. She saw the look on my face. "Father is not black he is white he has a dark tan. You see those blue eyes of his. Mother has brown eyes." Yes, their father was the most exotic man I had ever seen but he really did look black and Rashad looked just like their father. Their mother was gorgeous Rebecca took after her red hair and curvaceous body also. "So that is mother and father." I think that Rebecca had more than just that glass of wine because her words were kind of slurring. I could tell she was drunk. "They are a beautiful." I told her as she sat down. "Anyways one summer when I was seventeen and Bruce was sixteen, he got in a fit saying that he wanted to go to Atlanta. We did not see why because he did not like Rashad. Mother told me to stay in Wisconsin and to allow my brother to go and then I could go before the summer ended so that he could spend time with Father. She knew that if I went Bruce would have gotten no attention and he would have been upset. I obliged because I could spend time with my friends Giselle and Jessica." Tears started to form in her eyes. I went and sat next to her. "What is wrong? Rebecca?" She looked at me and I knew that she had experienced some pain. "Bruce had a friend Johnny and I liked Johnny I thought he was cute. Johnny was the bad boy type, so my mother always told me to stay away from him and Johnny did not seem to like me much anyways. Well Bruce had come back from Atlanta only two days of being there throwing a fit about Father loving Rashad more than him. We did not know what that was about, but I was pissed. I could have went on my trip. About a week after that everyone was gone. Giselle had stayed the night with me, and I stayed at home while Mom, Larry, Rick and Tyler went fishing. Bruce never did anything as a family, so he stayed back. We were sitting on the porch and Giselle asked me how I felt about not seeing my Father this summer. I did not know that Bruce was listening or that his friends were on their way to our house. I told Giselle that I was pissed, and that Bruce was a whiny little bitch. I meant what I said but I did not think that Bruce would have heard me." The look at in Rebecca's eyes made me not want to know more, but I needed to know what Bruce was capable of. "What happened?" "Twenty minutes later we were in my room and the door bust open. Bruce, Johnny, Carl, Randolph, David, James, and Steve pull Giselle and I out of the house. At first, I thought that Bruce was just trying to scare us, but I was wrong. He took us to the woods and tied us up. So, he said to me I am a whiny bitch. That is when I knew he had heard me. I thought okay maybe they are going to throw stones and things at us, but I was wrong. They raped us Johnny, Carl, Randolph, David, James, and Steve all raped me while Bruce watched." I was in shock and this was his sister and he did this to her. I could not believe what I was hearing. "After they raped me Bruce, Johnny, Randolph, Carl, David, James, and Steve raped Giselle and Bruce made me watch and he said now since you want to call me a whiny bitch watch this bitch whine." Tre was sitting there in shock I could see it in his eyes. I could not believe this was the man that I had been laying with. I was happy that he had not gotten a chance to do anything to Deena because I am sure he would have. He raped and tortured his sister, so I know he did not give a fuck about me. He did not care about anyone he was evil just like they had been telling me. He was a good pretender, but I was glad that I knew now. Rebecca was shaking as she relived the moment and I tried to console her, but it was like she was in a trance she pushed my arm away and continued. "Once they raped Giselle they started pissing on her and Bruce forced my mouth open and pissed in my mouth. He hit me over the head with a rock and I was out cold. I woke up delirious. I did not know how long I had been out, but I woke up in a hospital bed. I was talking about the devil and about demons. I was talking about Bruce. They medicated me so much that I could not even tell them what happened it was not until five years later that I told my story to Rashad." "What happened to Giselle?" Tre asked I had forgotten that he was still here he was so quiet. I knew her story was unbelievable to him as it was to me. "She went crazy too and she killed herself six months later. She was my world and she was my best friend. I keep her with me wherever I go." She pointed to the angel with wings tatted on her shoulder with Giselle's name on top of it. "Ugh I always get emotional when I tell people that story." She dried her eyes. "But I am strong now they did not bring me down and they did not defeat me Rashad taught me that. Rashad would travel all the way to Wisconsin to visit me while I was in the mental institution. He would talk to me he would comb my hair he would make sure I was okay." Tears dropped from her eyes and my eyes as well. "It was not until one day that Bruce tried to commit suicide I snapped out of my comatose state. I told Rashad everything." Damn Bruce tried to commit suicide I could not believe it. He seemed as if he was so happy but deep down inside, he was a scared little man. I could not believe that he could do something so cruel to his sister I knew he was a bad person. I just did not know how bad I wanted to know more I wanted to know how he had changed.

Chapter Fourteen
ANIYA

———————◦◦≫※◦※◦※◦◦———————

We decided to take a break and get something to eat. All the things that Rebecca was telling me was a bit much, I had to take it all in. I went upstairs into the bathroom and decided to call Rashad. He did not answer so I left him a voicemail. "I am so happy that you told me to come see your sister she is telling me good things about you. I want to see you again I really miss you." I smiled as I thought about all the things told me about Rashad. I hung and made my way back downstairs. Rebecca had made chicken and rice and some type of vegetable I had never eaten before and I was not going to eat it now. I think she told me it was eggplant. The kids were full, and I could tell they were tired. Mya took them upstairs to one of Rebecca's room while I stayed and continued to talk. "Rebecca how did you get over what happened to you?" I asked as she finished her wine. "Get over it honey please I will never get over it. The only reason why Bruce wants me to run the business that you guys own together is because he feels guilty." She waved her arms around. "You want to know how I have this huge house that is worth $2.5 million?" I nodded my head I did want to know. "Well Randolph is a heart surgeon who does not want to be outted, Carl is the Alderman in Wisconsin, Steven runs a billion-dollar design company for video games. Hell, they all are rich they were born into money. David runs a chain of fast food restaurants on the East Coast, and James play professional baseball for the Boston Red Sox. Yeah and they all pay me even Bruce." She sipped from her glass she had had been through so much. "What about Johnny what ever happened to him?" I noticed she didn't mention him. "He was killed by some woman's husband so he could not pay me. He didn't have shit any way but his mother was paid. Johnny was a loser! He was sleeping with this woman Destiny Gold you know the model." "Wow are you serious?" I did know her she was beautiful. She was older than us now, but she was a gorgeous woman. "Yes, he was sleeping with her and her husband who was an NFL player came home early one day and killed Johnny. Destiny lied and said that Johnny raped her and that is what got her husband off." "When you told Rashad, what happened what did he do?" "He found Bruce and beat his ass. Bruce and I were in the same mental hospital. I saw him one day and it triggered the memory. I started screaming, crying, and they could not calm me. They had to sedate me. They had called Rashad and he came. I cried as I told him everything that I remembered. He left that day and beat the shit out of Bruce. The people had to call the police on him. My mind focused on Rashad and getting him out of jail. I discharged myself and bailed him out. I did get through it. I did get back to reality. Although I still think about it every day and every night. I still want to kill Bruce but what would that help I would be locked away again at least I have my life and I am getting paid. All I have to do is make one phone call and I could have anything I want." She looked down at her feet and then her voice got quiet. "Well almost anything because they raped me so bad, I cannot have children. My husband says he doesn't want any children anyways." "Oh, so you are married I was thinking like this woman lives by herself in this big ole house?" "Well I do right now my husband is incarcerated. I spend my time working and volunteering. I have lots of free time right now but once he gets out it is back to the swing of things." I was happy that Rebecca could get on with her life after that horrific event. I could not believe that Bruce was so coldhearted. Just as he popped into my head, I got a text from him. Bruce 'Hey sexy.' I ignored his text. I thanked Rebecca for everything. It was late but we was going to make our way back home. After taking in all the information from her I had a plan. We packed the kids in the car and hit the highway. We were quiet as we all sat in our thoughts. We made it back to my house to find a squad car in front of my house. I did not know what had happened, but it scared me. Tre hopped out of the SUV and walked over to the car. Mya, the kids, and I sat in the truck holding our breath. Tre hurried back to the car and he did not look worried. "What is going on?" I wanted to know. "Lawrence came to the station with some information." He said and I was surprised. "I am going to go to the station and see what he is talking about and I will let you know. I think that you should go to Mya's house though just in case Chiquita is on some crazy shit." The man in the squad car came inside with us while I packed the kids and I some clothes. He introduced himself as Ray Bentley he was a handsome young cop. I went to the back and packed our clothes and hurried to leave. I left my car just so people would think we were at home. As I slid into Mya's car my phone dinged with a message from Bruce. Bruce 'oh bitch you can't answer my text?' He had lost his mind and I was not trying to help him find it. What I was trying to do was get my ass away from him. Too much was going on. I had Chiquita who was a killer and I was allowing her to keep my kids. I still had not talked to Cedes who had tried to set me up after she killed Vanessa. Then there was all this shit I had found out about my boyfriend Bruce and on top of that Rashad had not called me back. We made it to Mya's house and settled in for the night. The kids and I slept in her guest room. It started to rain and that made more uneasy. I hated when it rained it felt like the world was being washed away but there was forever going to be blood shed on Earth. Tre had not come back or called us and I was worried. All that worrying you would think that I would not sleep. Instead I slept through the night and woke up to an empty bed and the smell of food cooking. I looked down at my phone and it was on fifteen percent and I had a text message. I hope it was not Bruce and it wasn't. Rashad 'I need you here with me.' I felt the same way I needed him to be here with me too, but I needed to get everything straighten out. I sent him a kissy face to let him know I was thinking about him and powered off my phone to let it charge. I went to use the bathroom and then headed to the kitchen to see what there was to eat. I was hoping that Tre had called Mya or something. When I made it to the kitchen, I was pleased to see him sitting at the table. I made me a plate and we ate in silence. I knew Tre had to tell me something, but he did not want to say it in front of the kids. The anticipation was killing me, and I rapidly ate my breakfast. Mya grabbed the kids and took them to the back to watch cartoons. They were out of earshot and Tre was ready to tell me what I needed to hear. "We got her ass," he was talking about Chiquita. "Lawrence came in to tell us everything. He told us that Chiquita knew that he was dating Cedes hell she had set it up that way. She wanted to cause problems in their relationship. Apparently, Vanessa had tried to commit suicide before when Cedes had threatened to leave her. That was their plan to make Cedes want to leave Vanessa and cause Vanessa to commit suicide. What end up happening that day is Lawrence told Cedes that he was ready to be with her. Well Cedes had a change of heart and wanted to stay with Nessa. She goes to the hotel and tells Lawrence and comes back home. Nessa tells her that she doesn't want to be with her and Cedes loses it and kills her." "But that does not at all implicate Chiquita so what did you guys arrest her for?" Tre gave me the strangest look that it scared the damn hairs off my head. "Well we haven't arrested her yet, but we are for the premeditated murder of you. She was plotting to kill you we found a bomb under your car." My eyes got wide and I passed out. I was running in the field and a black crow was chasing me. I was running hard and fast and I was sweating. I was crying and running but I had plenty of energy, but the water was plunging down my face like a river. I did not know how I had all this energy with all these emotions swirling inside of me. I was tired. I made it to the end of the field the sunset was beautiful. That beautiful orange mixed with that yellow was like the Earth uniting with Heaven. I knew that I was going to win the race because after the sunset a rainbow raised out of the darkness. The rainbow rose without there being any rain. Except there had been rain the storm was me, it was within me, and since I had pushed so hard and kept going, I created a rainbow. The rainbow had come from inside of me.

Chapter Fifteen
ANIYA

⟫⟩⦿⟨⟪

I woke up to the sun shining through my window it was hot and my head hurt. I faintly remember what had happened and I know I needed answers. I did not know why Chiquita wanted to kill me, but I was happy that we had drove Mya's car instead of mine. My thoughts went to Deena and Malcolm, she had put my kids in jeopardy, I was going to pay that bitch back. Nothing mattered when it came to my kids, no one was going to endanger them. I got up threw on some black jogging pants and a white tee shirt I was about to find her and fuck her up. I do not know what had happened last night but today I was feeling better. To think this bitch had put a bomb under my car now what if my kids were in the car with me. I assumed she wanted to kill them too and that infuriated me even more. I walked out into Mya's hallway and seen that everyone was sleep what was going on? I looked at my phone and saw that it was six o'clock in the morning. Good I would surprise that bitch Chiquita. I saw that I had a text from Bruce calling me another stupid bitch because he had not heard from me. Oh, so I was a stupid bitch I would show him the stupid bitch I could be. After I fucked Chiquita up, I would go whoop Bruce's ass next. I was tired of taking all this bullshit lying down. I stole Mya's key off the table and got in her car. She had a blue 2014 Chevy Malibu. She had yet to upgrade but it still drove like a dream. The entire ride to Chiquita's house the only thing that was going through my mind was the question 'why did she want to kill me?' I did not understand it. I was done asking questions I was ready to take action. I climbed up the stairs to the apartment and was happy that her stupid ass still had not changed the locks. I creaked open the door and heard the shower running. She was in the shower that was perfect unless Lawrence was here. I quietly closed the door behind me. I crept to her room to make sure Lawrence was not there. If he was, I was ready to beat his ass too. Thankfully he wasn't it was just us. I was kind of hungry, so I went to check the refrigerator to see what she had in there. She had some leftover fish looked like Tilapia, some angel hair pasta and some garlic bread. I do not like leftover fish so that was a no go. I wonder how long she was going to be in the shower. I saw a fruit tray and grabbed a couple grapes. I decided to just eat an apple and sit and wait for her. She was taking all day. I guess she had to wash all that fat she had on her body. I heard the bathroom door open and Chiquita walked in her room singing a gospel song "Take Me to the King" by Tamela Mann the nerve of this evil bitch. Today was the day that she might just make it to The King. I was going to give her the surprise of her life. She was getting dressed and I sat in her living room waiting for her. Finally, she walked in. She saw me and jumped from shock. "Damn girl how the hell you get in here?" I threw down my spare key on her round coffee table. "I let myself in." I said and got up. She looked scared but at the same time mad she snatched up the keys and looked at them. "So, you let yourself in my shit?" She spat. This was the Chiquita I knew. I could see the fire in her eyes. I knew she hated me from when Hakeem died, and she was harassing me. But once we talked things over her hatred seemed to die down. Now I knew the truth it was a mask to get close to me.

"No, I let myself in my shit!" I yelled she had taken my home and now she was trying to take my life. She looked a bit shocked because we were on good terms. She could see I was not playing any games with her. "What the fuck do you want? I have not seen my niece and nephew in so long. What do you want I do not have time for this shit." She said. "You want to kill me bitch?" I asked. She smirked and that let me know that she was. Fuck it I punched her in her face and stepped back. I was done playing around. She looked shocked but she got herself ready and she swung and hit me in my chest. Her hit was weak all she had was fat no muscle. I hit her twice in the face with my right and punched her in her face one more time with my left. She stumbled back. She charged at me and knocked me onto the couch. She was on top of me and I continued hitting her in her head. I finally got enough room and pushed her off of me and she fell into the table. It was a sturdy wooden table because it held up against all her weight. I hurriedly ran to her body and started kicking her. She was doubled over in pain and I knew she was done for. She moaned out in pain and like Mortal Kombat I had to finish her. I grabbed a lamp and threw it at her body. She was out but she was not dead. I left out of the apartment and headed to Bruce's house. He lived about fifteen minutes away. I was tired of him, he kept leaving me fucked up messages on my phone calling me bitches and all types of stuff I was sick of him. He wanted to see an ignorant bitch in action then he would see one. I saw Mya calling me, but I ignored her call I was on a mission. I made it to his house, but I did not see his car. I called him and did not get an answer. I went and rang the doorbell and did not get an answer. Fuck it I went to the back of the house and took a rock and busted out the window of the door. I unlocked the door from the inside. After screaming his name and surveying the entire house it was clear that he was gone. I was going to show him what a real bitch could do. I took the balls of the pool table and threw them at his windows they shattered. I went to the refrigerator and grabbed the ketchup, mustard, hot sauce, and barbeque sauce and I made my way upstairs. I poured all the condiments in the middle of his bed and laid his comforter back across his bed so that he could not see it. I turned on every light in his house and turned on every faucet in his house. However long it took for him to come home that was how much it was going to cost him oh well his water and light bill would be going up. To add to it fuck it I turned on the heat. It was summertime and I knew this would be great his house would be hot damn near as hot as me. He had a chocolate cake on the counter. GREAT! I grabbed that chocolate cake and smeared it over his floors in the kitchen and his living room floor it looked like shit. I laughed he loved that beige carpet he had throughout his house. The times he told me my kids could not come over because he did not want them to waste anything on his floor. It made me feel good fucking up his shit, I grabbed his flour and threw it all over his house as much as I could get and when I ran out of flour. I found his body powder and produced a white cloud. I went to his television and ordered ten movies just or the hell of it, fuck him. I left his house feeling better than I had felt in a while. I went back to Mya's house only to find the police at her house. Damn she had called the police on me for stealing her car. I got out the car and they arrested it me. The white brunette cop said to me my Miranda rights "you have the right to remain silent. Anything you say can and will be used against you in a court of law. You have a right to an attorney if you cannot afford an attorney one will be appointed to you. Do you understand these rights?" She asked I shook my head yes. Every time I get in trouble, I call someone but this time I did not I just sat in that cell and thought long and hard. I didn't want to call Mya because I had done her wrong by stealing her car. I thought

I was being taken away for stealing Mya's car, but no Chiquita had called the police on me for beating her ass. Well it was worth it. She had me fucked up she was trying to kill me, and I went and beat her ass and she was mad. This was unreal. To be honest I was tired of all the back and forth with Hakeem's family. I just wanted to leave Wisconsin and start a new life. I needed to get away. I was so tired of this life and drama. I decided it was time to make a phone call. I called Rashad he answered on the first ring. I was hoping that he was going to help me I was hoping that he was going to tell me everything was going to be okay. I was surprised to hear a woman's voice answer my call. "Hello Niya" she said in her stupid ass accent. "Italy where is Rashad?" I asked I did not have time for games I did not understand why she had his phone and why she had accepted my call. "Oh, he went out on a date with his little girlfriend." My heart stopped girlfriend when did he get a girlfriend? "What girlfriend?" I asked. "Oh, her name is Jackie and she is as cute as a button." I was hurt. I hung up the phone because I did not have anything else to say. I was in tears. I knew this man did not think of me as his girlfriend but still I thought we were at least friends. Hell, who was I kidding I wanted to be his girlfriend so yes, I was hurt; and I did not know what to do. That night I cried myself to sleep. They did not come and bother me about anything when I was locked up, they did not even ask me any questions. All I know was that the next afternoon Bruce came to get me out of jail. I did not know how he knew I was in jail or anything, but I was happy he had come. I started crying and I rested my head on his shoulder. While they had told me so much about Bruce, I was still happy to see him. I was happy to see anybody. My heart hurt from finding out my potential guy had a girlfriend he had forgotten about me so quickly. I got in his car and he took me to a hotel he told me that his house had gotten vandalized. I did not say anything because I was the one who had did it. I went and got in the shower and put on a robe since that was all I had. Bruce was acting pretty nice and I was grateful for that. I had not been able to charge up my phone and I really wanted to check on my kids. Bruce told me to calm down and he brought me a drink. I was happy for that I needed it. It took me all but three swallows to finish the drink and it took me all but three seconds to feel the effects. But these effects were too strong. I could feel myself losing consciousness. I tried to get up and fell back down. He had drugged me.

BRUCE

Thanks to Italy for telling me where I could find that bitch Niya. Man, she kept going to fucking jail what the fuck she was a true hood rat. I needed to get rid of that bitch. She had been ignoring my fucking phone calls and texts just like a true bitch. I was tired of her and I was going to get rid of her for good. Yup I had got a hotel and buttered the bitch up. I had to borrow the money from Teresa to get her out of jail. Teresa was pissed that I was getting her out of jail but once I had control of the companies it was going to be okay. Teresa gave me the money and then she told me to never call her again. I know my baby didn't mean it as soon as my plan went through, she was going to be putty in my hands. That bitch Aniya was so fucking dumb to come with me and drink something that I gave her. She fell out and I got my camera ready. I put my dick on her lips as she lie there. My dick was rock hard too so that helped. It was crazy though because her eyes popped open, so I hurriedly snapped the picture. I slapped that bitch and I heard her moan. She was out of it I laughed. I opened up her robe and took pictures of her naked body. I opened her shaven pussy it looked good. I licked the lips. Aniya always tasted good. I opened her legs and took a picture of her pretty pussy. I decided I might as fuck her for old times, sake. As she lay defenseless on the hotel couch, I pounded that pussy. It felt so good and the thought that she was helpless was even better. I came in five minutes. I had the power. I left her there in the hotel room and devised my plan. I went to lay low at Teresa's house. When I made it to the house, I saw that there was another car in front of her house. That pissed me off I just knew she was not fucking someone else. I started banging on the door loudly. "Teresa let me the fuck in before I act a fucking fool! You in there fucking!" My face turned red as I thought about her cheating on me. As soon as I said that the door swung open a black man stood there. He was dark as night with dark eyes. He was strong and looked scary. I didn't give a fuck though he wasn't going to punk me. He looked at me and he had his shirt off. I saw Teresa peeking behind him. "Oh, you fucking niggas now!" I snapped. The dude hit me in my face so hard I fell. I could hear myself snoring. Teresa started shaking me and I could barely understand what was going on. "You didn't have to do that Duane you didn't have to knock him to sleep. Bruce get up!" She shook me. I opened my eyes. "Are you okay?" "Man fuck you Teresa you need to get rid of that muthafucka before I hurt him." The guy said and rode away. Teresa helped me into the house. I checked to make sure I didn't have any bruises on my face I was straight. "Bruce we are done." Teresa told me. "What the fuck do you mean we are done?" "You heard me Bruce I am with Duane now." "The nigga!" I yelled this was not right. "Don't call him that asshole! He loves me I am with him and I am done with you" I started choking her before I knew it. I looked and I could tell she couldn't breathe. I couldn't kill her I loved her. I threw her frail body down on the floor and ran out the house. She would change her mind as soon as she found out what I had done. As soon as she realized I was going to be rich.

Chapter Sixteen
ANIYA

⟶ ⟫⟡⟨ ⟵

They had told me that they were looking for Bruce but there was nothing that the police could really do. He had not checked in under his name. He had a cap on so they could not really see his face it was my word against his. I did not understand how Bruce knew I was in jail. Tre said that the police was not pressing charges for Chiquita getting beat up and that they were really just holding me for my own safety. Mya and Tre knew where I was because he worked with the police but that still did not explain how Bruce knew where I was? Tre said that they had gotten Chiquita on tape confessing to trying to murder me using Lawrence. She would not get much time, but she would get some time. That time she would be in jail was enough for me to leave without a trace. Too much was going on and I still and I was not taking care of business. Mya said she had everything under control. She said I needed to move far away from Wisconsin like Paris and that is what made me think about it, Italy! I had called Rashad and told Italy that I was in jail and I bet she told Rashad. Damn I could not trust anybody. I thought I could, but I could not. I do not know what thrill Bruce had gotten out of raping me but we had still had these companies together. I was released from the hospital and I went back to Mya's house I did not want Bruce to find me at home. Susan had left me an urgent message, and so did Bertha I was going to call them after I got my rest. Rashad had been blowing up my phone with calls and texts. He kept asking me if I was alright was anything wrong. Yeah like he did not know he had me all the way fucked up. I felt like, he had set me up. Italy, Bruce, and Rashad could all go to hell for all I cared. Guilt hovered over my head like a cloud. I was not myself I knew it was karma paying me back for what I had done to Hakeem. He was beating on me, but I could have just left. I did not have to kill him, but we all make choices in life and that was my choice and I was dealing with the backlash from it. I was happy that my kids were not feeling it firsthand. I had not been able to spend time with them, but thankfully they did not know what was going on. I rested my eyes and fell asleep. I needed that rest. Tre was there with us just in case Bruce came back and I knew I had business to take care of in the morning. I had to see what Susan and Bertha wanted. I made my ways to Susan's office feeling groggy. I was back to my old haircut and I had bags under my eyes. I did not have on any make up or anything I just had on lip gloss. I put on some jeans and a shirt because I was not in a fashionable mood. The sun was hot that morning and it was only nine in the morning I knew it was going to be a scorcher. I made my way into the building and waited for Susan to allow me to come in. I had not called her back I just showed up and I knew she had other appointments. Whoever was there must not had been important as me because once she found out it was me, she hurried them out and called me in. I sat down and Susan got right into it. "What the fuck have you been doing?" She shot at me. I looked confused. She threw some images to me. I was butt naked on a couch. To be exact the hotel couch. I had a white penis on my lips, in my face and my eyes were open. I looked shocked in the picture. So that is what Bruce was doing he was taking pictures of me. He had my legs cocked open on one of the pictures with my shaven vagina open for everyone to see. Then she showed me the note sign over all businesses or these pictures will be on the internet. There was no name, but I knew it was Bruce. I started to explain everything to Susan. "Bruce drugged me. I went to jail which you know about for beating Chiquita up and he came and got me. We went to the hotel next thing I know I was laid out. Then I was in the hospital the housekeepers at the hotel had found me passed out." "Why Aniya? I told you not to get involved with this man." Susan said. She looked like she wanted to cry for me. I did not cry though I had been through too much for some pictures to bring me to some tears. "I don't know I was lonely." I said and that was the truth. "Let me tell you something and I want you to listen good. Just because you don't have anyone to lay next to you does not make you lonely. Just because you don't have a warm body next to you that does not make you alone. You are your best friend. We get ourselves in some fucked up situations because we want to feel someone next to us. Forget that we need to learn to be by ourselves." She started crying. I did not know why she was so emotional. "My husband left me." I got up and gave her a hug. She wiped her tears. "Just because I am crying that does not mean I am going to jump in another relationship though. I am crying because it hurts, and it is okay to hurt but we must all get over situations that happen to us instead of jumping into the next situation." "I thought I could trust Bruce," I tried to explain to Susan. "Bullshit, you jumped in a relationship quickly after Hakeem's death. I know it was because you did not want to be alone. That is fine sometimes if that other person mean you well but in order to know that you need to really dig deep because the face of the devil looks like an angel. You remember that." I sat there for a minute then I remembered I needed to call Bertha. "Hold on a second Susan I had a woman looking into some things for me and she called me also so let me give her a call." I dialed Bertha's number and it rang. She did not answer. As soon as I hung up, she was calling me back. I put her on speaker. "Bertha I am here with my lawyer Susan I have you on speaker. Bruce drugged me and took some messed up pictures of me naked. He said he was going to put them on the internet if I did not sign over the businesses so please tell me you got some good news." I said out of breath. "Oh, honey do not even worry about him because I found the key to all your answers." I listened while Bertha spoke, and I damn nearly wanted to fall out of my seat. I wanted to kiss her through the phone. The plan she came up with was so fantastic, but I needed a little insurance and I knew just who to call. I was lost this morning but now I had all the pieces to puzzle of my life. I was grateful I was given a second chance. When I got back to Mya's house, she was making lunch for the kids. I let them eat and then I took my kids to the lake. I needed to spend time with them. They were all I had. I sat at the lake on a rock and really thought about things. All the things I had been through in the last year were my fault. I wanted to be loved again so bad when the truth is Hakeem did not even love me right. I was slowly getting back to loving myself and I had allowed another idiot in my life. Although I oozed confidence and self-esteem, I knew that I was just another broken woman looking for love. I should have seen all the signs that Bruce was not the one for me. When I did see the signs, I used the businesses as an excuse to steady come back. In reality I could have just dumped him and figured out the business part on my own. He had disrespected me and said some harsh things about me, and I still went back using the "business" as an excuse. My companies were the things that I was desperately trying to hold on to but at the beginning I was ready to sell and move on. I was using the businesses as an excuse not to move on. I had let my kids down, my friend down, and myself down. I did need the money to live comfortably but truth be told I had over two million dollars in my savings account alone. I could take a loss and rebuild if needed too. Nevertheless, I knew that I was using those businesses as an excuse to hold on to Bruce.

To see if maybe my ears were deceiving me, how could someone not love me when I had a man who was taking care of me. That is the bullshit that really was leading my life those stupid ass thoughts. I needed to get real with myself. Men treated women like shit everyday no matter how beautiful they were, how nice their figure were, if a man did not love himself then he could not love a woman. I should have learned that with Hakeem but nope I didn't. Rashad was someone I could see myself with. I did not trust him, and truth be told I needed time to get myself back together. My kids were first priority, Deena and Malcolm. I loved them so much and I was steady showing them that their mother was not independent. I was happy they were young because I really wanted to make things up to them. We left the lake and I had a whole different aspect of life in front of me. I was going to face my fears and I was not going to let anyone deter my goals. I was a businesswoman I could do it alone. I did not need anyone to help me be a success I was a successful all on my own. Hopefully things were going to go good with Bruce and these contracts so and I was going to be okay. I did not feel like dealing with him anymore and hopefully I would not have too. I said a prayer that night something that I had not done in a long time, "Heavenly father watch over me and my children and friends. I repent for all the killings I have done for all the deceiving I have done. I am not perfect, but I will try in the future to be better. Keep walking with me Father God and shower the blood of Jesus over me to protect me to protect my children to protect my friends. Lead my heart into the good of the land instead of leading me into the weak. In Jesus name Amen." I was crying when I got finished. I had never asked for forgiveness when I killed Hakeem. I know deep down in my heart that I was wrong. I knew deep down in my heart that nothing about killing him was right. I am human and I made a mistake. I thought that was my only way out. I had no guidance I knew that was a problem I had. I always went with my first mind I never thought about things. I was deeply sorry that I had killed Hakeem. I know I showed no remorse, but I was sorry, and it hurt me to live without him. He was like that piece of chocolate that a diabetic knew they could not have but if they went without it, they would go crazy. Hakeem was not at all perfect, but I loved him just the same. He had rescued me and given me two precious kids. That was the most important thing he had given me the two most precious gifts on earth Malcolm and A'Deena.

Chapter Seventeen

ANIYA

———— ✦ ⟫⟪ ✦ ————

I met Bruce and Sampson at Sampson's office with Susan. They had the paperwork ready for me to sign. It was a Friday and I was going to visit Rashad as soon as I left the office. I needed to see what was going on with him. I wanted to know who the hell was Jackie? Plus, I had incorporated his business in this plot so I needed to let him know when everything worked out fine. I wanted to believe that he had not set me up and that he was a good guy I needed that to be true with all this evilness around me I needed a little good. We sat at the table and Bruce stared daggers at me. The bastard was looking at me like I had done something wrong to him. No longer did he look good to me, he looked ugly just like his soul. What he didn't know was that I was one step ahead of him, I was good, and I was about to be even better. Sampson took the paperwork out of his suitcase. Susan looked it over and looked at me, "are you sure you want to do this?" Damn she was playing her part. I looked sadly at Bruce, "yes at this point I just want this whole ordeal to be over." That was the truth. Bruce had a smirk on his face. "That's right you stupid bitch" he laughed. "No need for the language Bruce." Sampson told his client. I signed the documents where I needed and slid the papers back to Bruce. I looked sadly at him while he looked over the documents, I had to distract him. "Are you going to give me my pictures you fucking asshole!" I said and Susan gave me a slight tap. "What? I call it like I see it." She whispered, "be good." She did not know what I was doing but it worked Bruce looked up and started signing the papers and smiled at me. "Yes of course darling I am tired of looking at that body anyway." He said signing all the documents and talking shit. "You are one trifling hoe the way you spread that pretty pussy so that I could take flicks of it you liked that didn't you?" He laughed as he signed the last document. We got ourselves together and he handed Susan the pictures of me over to her. I was happy that everything was over. I needed to get the contract from Sampson so that I could have Rashad sign his part so that it could officially be just me and him. I was so happy that I had gotten this done and I was ready to take flight. Chiquita was locked away so I did not have to worry about her, and Mya and the kids would be going to Bertha's for the weekend. Bertha said she needed some company that was the least we could do since she had done this favor me. I hugged Susan after we left Sampson's office. "Thank you so much and I will never! I mean never! Ignore your warnings thank you for being there for me." I got in my car and I saw Bruce leaving out of the office. He threw his hand up and I threw my middle finger up. His stupid ugly ass made me sick to my stomach. I got my suitcase from the house and headed to the airport. I did not know what I was going to walk into when I got to Atlanta, but I was prepared for anything. I did not even call Rashad I was just going to show up. I had done some thinking and I was ready to take that leap with Rashad if he was willing too. That was all I needed. I had thought about just being alone, but why should I stop from falling in love because of some bad relationships. Rashad and I had chemistry that we just could not shake he knew this, and I knew it. Once I made it to Atlanta, I went to the car rental place to get my car. I headed to Rashad's place I remembered the way although

I had only been to Atlanta twice. As I got closer, I thought to myself that I should have called but it was too late. I parked in his driveway and his car was not there. I tried my luck and knocked on the door. There was no answer I knew that he was probably at the strip club. Damn I was not thinking I should have called first better late than never I decided to call now. It seemed like it took forever for him to answer the phone, but he did. "What up" he sounded pretty annoyed and I could not blame him I had not called him or replied back to him in a while. "I am sitting outside your house. Are you at the club if so send me the address." I got right to the point. Rashad started laughing. "You lying." Was his reply. I didn't respond to him. He got the point and gave me the address and I put it in the GPS. The entire ride there I was thinking about what I was going to say. I wanted to know who was Jackie and I also wanted to know if he told Bruce I was in jail. I pulled into the parking lot of the club and it had changed a bit. It was still black and blue, but it looked a bit cleaner. There was about a dozen cars in the parking lot. I got out the car and made my way to the front of the club. There was a big Suge Knight looking fella in front of the club I guess he was security. "Damn you must be new what's your name?" His southern accent was strong. I looked him up and down and shook my head. I was dressed kind of slutty. I had on some coochie cutter white shorts with a white halter top. I had my hair back short and I had a bit of blonde in it. I had done my makeup before I pulled off from in front of Rashad's house. I had on some silver heel sandals and my toes were manicured. I guess I could see how he thought I was one of the dancers. "I am Niya and I am looking for Rashad." He let me pass and uttered under his breath, damn. I knew he was looking at my ass. There was no one in the club. But I had noticed that Rashad had fixed the place up. It was nice too he had plasma televisions and he had updated the bar. The stage was updated and bigger I liked it. The Suge Knight look alike led me to the back and I had gotten a bit nervous if it was not for the cars hell, I would have thought he was trying to set me up. Good thing I had bought me a gun. Too many people hated me and wanted me dead I needed the protection. He walked me to the back to what looked like a conference room. When he opened the door, all eyes were on us. There were at least fifteen people in the room but the only person I cared about was Rashad. He was at the front of the room on the other side. Some people were standing up because there was not enough tables. Out of the fifteen people twelve of them were women and I could tell they were dancers. Italy was standing close to Rashad and she looked piss when she saw me. I sashayed my sexy ass to the front of the room. All eyes were on me and I know they wanted to know who I was. Rashad gave me a hug and you could tell the bitches were mad about that. As he wrapped his big strong arms around me, I inhaled his masculine scent. I damn near fell to the floor because he was making me weak. He let me go and I turned around to face everyone. "This right here is one of my business partners Aniya Turner. She came to see how well the club has flourished and where her money has gone." He started laughing. "Thank you for the introduction Rashad. I am actually the only business partner he has. "I said and turned towards him he smiled. "Anyways I do want to get to know each and every one of our employees but right now is not the time. I know Rashad has some things he wants to talk about." I stood next to Rashad and allowed him to finish his meeting. "Okay back to business we have not even been reopened for that long and you old dancers are up to y'all old bullshit. I made it very clear that there is no selling ass in this club. This is not a hoe house y'all sell pussy on y'all own time. Jackie stand up." He demanded. I waited intensely to see which girl was my competition. A long legged brown skinned beauty stood up. She had a long blue weave in her head and it really looked nice on her. You could tell her titties were bought they were perky and perfect. She had a nice flat tummy and I was a bit jealous. This was Jackie the bitch he was with that day. I wanted to beat her ass and let her know that I was number one. I didn't feel like making a fool of myself today, so I stood there quietly. "Here," he walked over to her and handed her a pink slip. "You are fired." She looked at him in disbelief." "What the fuck Shad, like why the fuck am I getting fired are you for real?" Jackie twisted her face up. Rashad did not say anything back the Suge Knight looking security and the other security who had been in the corner came and grabbed her. She was kicking and screaming and talking shit. "This goes to show y'all that I am not playing with nobody. Jackie was the best money maker in this muthafucka. Yeah she liked to suck my dick too." My eyes got big he was telling too much information. "I do not give a damn about none of that shit. This here is my business!" He walked behind me and wrapped his arms around me. "This here is our business let me correct myself and no one is about to fuck our money up. All that prostitution shit you hoes hop on back page because my ladies are trying to get this money the right way." I could tell that some of the women were happy that Jackie was gone but there was this one particular chick who had a red straight weave in. She was a redbone like me she seemed to have an attitude. Rashad must have picked up on it too because he pointed her out "Peaches you mad because your home girl gone? You got something to say?" "Naw Rashad but you didn't have to do her like that. You know she fucked with you." She looked at me. She was ugly and her teeth was kind of messed up and overlapped. "Don't play me Peaches I know she was trying to fuck with me to get in my head like she did Al's ass. That was not about to happen to me. Look at me baby girl." He let me go and walked up to her. "I ain't no conceited ass nigga but I know I am good looking. You pull that shit with them old no hoe getting ass niggas out there don't pull that shit with me." He said. Damn Rashad was showing me another side of him and I was starting to rethink the entire trying to get with him thing. I just stood there in silence. If he was talking to these women like that then how in the hell would he talk to me someone he knew had slept with his brother. "Well damn," Peaches replied to him. "You are the bottom of the barrel not because of your looks but mainly because of your attitude. We are in Atlanta this ain't Magic City, but we will get there if you learn to get your shit together. I am trying to mold you guys come on." His tone got calmer and he became the Rashad I remembered. "Let's get this money and build a reputable club so that we could get more money." He told everyone that they could leave it was just him, Italy, and I. He turned to Italy "you can go." He said she rolled her eyes. He waited for her to leave and he walked up to me and kissed me passionately. This was the Rashad I longed for. He grabbed my ass and smacked it. "Hi to you too," I giggled once he let me go. "We are the only business partners, huh?" "Did you tell Bruce that I was in jail?" I blurted out.

Chapter Eighteen
RASHAD

I was happy when my baby Aniya walked in. It was a good surprise and her ass was looking right in those damn little ass shorts. I know niggas was looking. She had lost some weight, but that ass was still fat. I wanted to lay her down and put my face in that wet pussy. We had to clear somethings up first. When she asked me did, I tell Bruce that she was in jail I was confused. I didn't even know she was in jail. "I was in jail did Italy tell you?" She asked me. "You was in jail when?" I asked I couldn't believe she was locked up. She went on to explain that Italy had answered my phone and told her that I was with Jackie. I could see the hurt on her face when she said that. Jackie didn't mean shit to me and I wanted to explain but Aniya wasn't done talking. She told me about the things that Bruce did to her in the hotel. I was beyond pissed. My blood was boiling. "Damn I did not know all this shit was going on!" I told her. "So if you didn't tell Bruce who did?" She asked like I had an answer for her. Then she looked like she had the answer to life. "Italy! I am about to tear her ass in half!" She stormed off. I was right behind her as we walked through the club. I had some food catered and the rest of the employees were eating but we did not know where Italy was. I called out to my security Liam. "Liam! Where Italy go?" I asked. "She went out to her car." Liam said. Niya didn't say shit as she made her way to the door. She was pissed I could see that. The entire club was following behind us as we went outside. Niya turned to me. "What car she in Rashad?" "Aye everybody go back inside," I said. Liam took that as his cue to navigate the crowd. Once everyone was back in I let her know that Italy was in a red Impala. Niya made her way to the red Impala that Italy was in and she was talking on the phone. I suspected she was talking to Bruce. Whoever it was she hung up on them. Niya was standing there looking cool I didn't know what was about to happen. Italy opened the door smiling. Before we knew what was happing Niya pulled her out the car and punched Italy in the face. "Bitch you set me up." She punched her again. "No, no, no!" Italy yelled she hit the floor and Niya kicked her in the face. Italy wasn't even trying to fight back. "Calm down Niya let's see what is going on first." I pulled Niya off Italy. Niya kicked her again and turned to leave. I helped Italy up to make sure she was good. I had to get to the bottom of this shit.

ANIYA

Everyone was looking when we made it the club. You could tell they wanted to know what was going on. I walked to the back where we had just left, Rashad dragged the bitch through the club. As soon as we got in the room Rashad was on her ass. "What the fuck is going on?" Rashad yelled at Italy who was sitting in the chair crying. "Shut that shit up Lee man what the fuck is going on!" "I am fucking Bruce! That is what is going on!" She yelled. I was shocked. This bitch was a hoe and she was fucking my man while he was my man. I punched the bitch again just because she had the nerve to say that shit to my face like I had not just been with Bruce. "Nobody gives a fuck why the fuck is you telling Bruce Niya's business and lying and shit. You know what the fuck I am talking about. Now what the fuck is going on?" Rashad yelled. I did not know Rashad had this gangster side to him. It was a turn on though for some reason. "I have been sleeping with Bruce and I told him that Niya was in jail that day. I did not know what he was going to do I just told him." "Why the fuck did you tell me Rashad was with Jackie? Why didn't you tell him I was calling him!" I yelled. "He was with Jackie." Italy said and looked at Rashad. Rashad avoided eye contact with me. It was true and it hurt my feelings, but I took it. "I did not feel like telling Rashad that you was in in jail him." She said with an attitude. "Bitch!" I said running towards her, but Rashad stopped me. "You was on the phone calling Bruce to tell him Niya was here with me?" Rashad asked. She shook her head yes "he did not answer though." I shook my head at Italy I didn't understand what she got out of keeping track of me. The bitch was obsessed. "Are you sure!" Rashad yelled and it scared me. She shook her head yes. "You know damn well that I could end you right now don't you Italy?" He had a daunting tone. I got afraid what was he talking about he could end her. "You do not make any calls and you hurry your ass out of here and I bet not ever see you." "What about Darien?" She asked in tears. "I will explain everything to him. You have to fucking go!" He demanded.

She jumped up and hurried out the door. I did not know what had just happened, and I was not sure if we were safe. "Do you think that she will tell Bruce that I am here?" I asked. I was not scared of Bruce, but I just did not want any surprises. My plan was still in motion and I did not want anything to deter Bruce. "Naw," he said shaking his head no. He turned to me and smiled. "Look at you." He said putting his arms around my waist and bringing me close to him. "You smell good too. Who the hell told you to wear those little ass shorts." I laughed. "I was trying to wear them for you." "I hear you but don't do it again. I don't want men to see what belongs to me." He said smacking my ass again. "I belong you now is that right?" I asked. "Hell, yeah you been mine I just needed you to handle that situation with Bruce so did you handle it?" "Yes," I grabbed the piece of paper out of my purse. It was the contract to the strip club. My plan had worked perfectly. The plan was complex yet simple. I would sign the papers that he wanted signing, but I signed where he was supposed to sign. He signed where I was supposed to sign so in other words, he had signed his half away. Sampson his lawyer had known what was going down too. Sampson was an old head and he knew of Bertha, Cedes's mother. After their father had went to prison Bertha had started a whore house. She had been a whore herself there and she had become rich off her pussy. Well I promised Sampson one night of pleasure with the famous Black Love. I had done my research. I found out that Sampson was having problems in the bedroom and Bertha could help. Although she had stopped hoeing, she was still giving men advice on how to please their woman. She gave women advice on how to please their man. Sampson was so happy that he would not have to pay to get help that without hesitation he agreed to help me. He had highlighted the wrong parts on purpose, and he knew what was going on. I was happy that this plan had worked out. That night in Atlanta we partied with our employees. I must admit this was my first time in a strip club. I was just as excited as the men. The place had gotten packed around eleven o'clock and I had about five drinks. It was safe to say I was drunk. I was amped up with everyone else. I was dancing and the men thought I was a dancer. Rashad grabbed my arm and made me sit down I guess I was getting a bit out of control. I was making it rain on the girls. I was having the time of my life. I had not enjoyed myself in so long that I had forgotten what it was about. There was a point in my life when I did not enjoy myself. I was an abused woman who had won the battle. For years

I had been trapped inside my home, inside my body. Now here I was a bit slimmer and enjoying myself. I had so much money that I could not even imagine how to spend it. On top of that I had two beautiful babies, I was living my best life. I was on top and I was making money on my own. Rashad had a look in his eyes as I stood up and shook my ass. It was the same look that Hakeem had given me a million times. The look like he wanted to whoop my ass. I didn't think that Rashad was a woman beater, but those type of men never came with warning labels. I wasn't worried about it. If it came down to it I would fight or kill before I let a man hit me. I was living in the moment and I needed for him to be living in it too. I walked over to him and started shaking my ass on him. He just stood there looking. I liked Rashad and I needed to know that he was the one. I turned to him. "I need for my man to have fun with his girl. Don't be so uptight." He was still looking serious, but he did at least grab my hips. I stayed dancing on him all night. I guess I could calm down and only dance on him. I was just having so much fun.

Chapter Nineteen
ANIYA

It was the end of the night and we had to wait for everyone to leave. Liam could see that we wanted to be alone so he told Rashad that he would close up. I could tell he was also enjoying the stripper Lucky. I think he was trying to take her down. Rashad had rode with Italy to the club, so he rode back with me. We made it to his house, and everything was in place when we walked in. I wonder what he had on Italy that she would disappear like that. "Do you think she told Bruce I was here?" I asked as we made our way up the stairs. "No, you ain't got to worry about that." He said as we went to his room. Rashad started getting undressed and I liked the view. We took separate showers, but I still wanted to know about Italy. I had talked to Mya and she said they were having fun. I was happy because I damn sure was having fun. Rashad got in the bed with me and we cuddled. "So why are you so sure that Italy will not tell anything?" I wanted to know. "My brother is in jail with her brother Cedric. They are doing their bid together and my brother is running shit in there. A chick he knows is the CO in the jail and she helps him bring in all types of illegal shit. Italy know that if she fuck up that Cedric is dead. Shit her entire family will be dead. Italy has three children who live with her mother. She knows who my brother Darien is, and she knows that he will order a hit without hesitation if I need him too. She has seen it done." Wow I was lost for words I did not know that Rashad had it like that. "Well how is he going to take that his fiancé has disappeared?" "He was never going to marry that bitch! He married to Rebecca already." Rashad told me. "Rebecca? Your sister?" I asked. "Yeah shit they not related they are married. Rebecca runs a lot of shit. Hell, she is the head of Darien's operation." I smiled I guess she was the perfect person to call for what I needed. I was happy that she was on my side. "Rebecca gets much respect did she tell you what happened to her?" I shook my head yes. "That was some foul ass shit that Bruce did to let some niggas rape your sister. He is a sick muthafucka." "He is so why the hell you didn't tell me?" "Like I told you before it ain't my story to tell. Plus, hell I was trying to push up on you so I knew you would not have taken me serious." That did make sense to me. I would have probably told him he was lying and stayed with Bruce and none of this would have happened. I would have signed my businesses over and would not have shit to show for it. "Let's take a picture." He leaned in a kissed me and we took a picture. I stuck out my tongue and we took another picture. I loved every moment of this silly stuff we were doing. I liked Rashad and I was happy that he liked me back and was not up to no games. I needed someone who could be real with me. I was hoping that it would be Rashad. I sent the pictures and sent them to their destination. "Who you texting?" Rashad asked over my shoulder. I had turned my body. "Nobody important." I said and snuggled up next to this man who was so loving and trusting that I was scared that I would wake up from this dream. At first, I was ready to move away just me and the kids but in reality, I really did want someone. I was so used to having someone that was all wrong for me that this time I was hoping that Rashad was right for me. I knew that my uncertainty was due to the fact that I was always in bad situations. This time it felt like this was going to be something different, something special. The next morning, I made Rashad breakfast and we conversed about all the things that we wanted in the future. Rashad said that he had a son Rashad Junior whom he had not seen since he was born. I was hoping that I could help him find him. He said his baby mama Talia had ran off with some man after the baby was born. I knew it was more to the story and I was hoping that he would tell me when he felt the need to. I told him I had gotten my tubes tied. He did not seem to be discouraged by that. When he asked me about Hakeem and his death, I told him about Hakeem beating on me. I told him about how he belittled me in front of people. I told him how he ran my life and how I was afraid for my life. As he sipped his orange juice he asked. "How did he die again?" I looked at him to see if I could trust him. I wasn't certain that I could. "An asthma attack," I said and put my head down. "Damn an asthma attack? Why didn't you help him find his inhaler?" "He was beating my ass I was scared I didn't know he was having an asthma attack." I wanted to tell him the truth, but some things are better when you keep them to yourself. "Yeah okay and the police believed that shit?" Rashad laughed. "What do you mean that was the truth." I was offended. "Okay Niya I see you girl." He laughed. He went and washed the dishes. He told me to get dressed and he was taking me out. We had gone to the Zoo the last time I was here in Atlanta with him. I was sad that I was here without the kids I definitely wanted to show them different things. I called and checked up on them. Mya said her, Tre, and Bertha were taking the kids to an amusement park that sounded fun. I was so happy that Mya cared so much about my kids and I hoped she got blessed with her own kids one day. I got dressed in my white sundress with my yellow heels. I was cute and Rashad saw what I had on and went in this closet. He pulled out some white shorts and a yellow and blue shirt. He had some yellow and blue shoes to match. I thought that was adorable that we were matching. "We look good together," Rashad said. I agreed we did look good together better than Bruce and I had ever looked. We got in his Hummer and set out for our destination. He would not tell me where we were headed. We drove for what seemed like forever and we stopped at a beautiful brick house. There were about five cars out on the street. I looked at

Rashad where was he taking me? He didn't even knock he just walked right in. "Ma!" Aw shit he was taking me to meet his mother. I had never met any man's mother before. I wish he would have told me before so that I could have told him no. I knew that was probably why he did not tell me. We headed to the back of the house where there was another entrance to the backyard. The kitchen was hot I guess from the oven being on. It smelled good in there. He guided me into the backyard where there were a couple of people. They were older people I was guessing they were his parents' friends. I spotted his mother standing next to someone who I guessed was his father. She seen us and her eyes lit up but then they dimmed. I wonder what she was thinking. We walked over to her hand in hand. Rashad kissed her cheek but her beautiful eyes were looking at me. She was pretty just like the picture I saw of her. "What up Pops.?" Rashad said to the man who was grilling. It was the man from the pictures. "Who is this Rashad?" His mother intervened looking me up and down. "Ma this my fiancé Niya." He introduced me as his fiancé was, he crazy? "Well I don't see a ring on her finger." She said and I was growing nervous his mother was still looking at me. I on the other hand was sitting there smiling like a damn fool. "That's cause I haven't asked her yet but when I do, she gone say yes. She gone be my fiancé." He said wrapping his arms around me. I guess this would be the perfect time to speak up. "Hello Mrs.Thompson," I stuck out my hand. She did not stick hers back she just looked at me again. "Umph and y'all are matching." She was not impressed as she rolled her eyes and walked away. Damn she was one tough cookie I was going to have to crumble I just did not know how. "Don't even worry about her honey she will grow on you." Rashad's father said, "I am Brandon Thompson. Rashad's father nice to meet you honey." He walked around and hugged me. He did something and I think that he was looking at my butt. Rashad laughed and I knew for sure he was. Renee, Rashad's mother asked if anyone wanted to help her bring out the side dishes to put on the outdoor burners. I told her I would, and she rolled her eyes and said come on. When I walked in the kitchen, she had everything already prepared. I started grabbing the stuff without even saying anything because I really did not know what to say. To be honest I did not care for his mother and her nasty attitude. I was almost done, and she had not said a word to me I came back into the kitchen. "Do you have any kids?" She asked. "Yes, two a boy and girl A'Deena and Malcolm." I said. "How old are they?"

She questioned. "Malcolm is seven and Deena is five." "Okay so what do you do for a living?" She asked as she poured herself a glass of wine. "I am a businesswoman. I own part of a hair salon, a cleaning company, I also buy houses, rebuild them and sell them and I also own a portion of Rashad's club." She seemed a bit impressed. "Sounds like a great resume. Do you love my son?" "Yes, I guess." I said. "Well look here if you want to be a part of this family you need to be sure that you love him because I will not play about my son." She kind of screamed but it was low. I did not know who this woman thought she was talking to. I did not have to be sure of shit. I did not have to prove myself to her I wanted to be with her son and not her. "I will not play about my feelings neither. I am a mother too who has a son so I can understand the aggression. You don't know me, but I bet if you got to know me you would like me if you gave me a chance." She rolled her eyes. "Give you a chance shit you better be glad you eating my food. Now go take that food outside." I didn't even say anything I just took the rest of the food outside. When I was finished, I went and sat by Rashad I did not have time for his mother's bullshit. She had some nerve coming at me like that. From the moment she seen me with her son she had an attitude. I did not know what was up with her, but she had better calm down because hell I beat up old people too.

RASHAD

I saw Moms giving Niya a hard time. She always did bullshit like that. I knew that Niya was tough though. She handled Mr. Richards and Bruce in that damn meeting, and I loved that about her. She did not back down business wise and I knew she could be my trap queen. She looked so soft and delicate. I did not know if she could handle all of me. I was willing to take that leap of faith with her. was throwing a party shit I was just there. Jeremih's "Birthday Sex" came on and I saw Niya swaying her hips from across the room. My Pops old ass friend Curly was eyeing my lady. I made my way over to her. I mugged his old ass I didn't give a damn about him being old and my Pops friend I would beat his ass. I put my arms around her waist. "Your sexy ass better stop winding your hips like that." I whispered in her ear. She smiled. I could tell Niya was in love with me. She had never experienced a nigga like me. I was a fucking boss and I was going to need a boss lady like her by my side. I slow grinded with my baby I was going to love her and her kids like they were my own. My baby mama had ran off with my son a while ago with her stupid ass. I didn't know where they were at currently, but I was looking for her. I couldn't focus solely on her right now. I was going to have a new life with Aniya and her kids.

Chapter Twenty
ANIYA

I thought that Rashad's mother would never accept me. Later in the day she finally calmed her nerves probably because of all those damn drinks she had. She even took pictures with me. She was laughing and acting like we were old school friends. Her friends were cool too. The party was for her friend's Valerie ten-year anniversary. Ten-years of what I was not sure, but Rashad's mom was the life of the party. She pulled me to the side during a dance and had a nice chat with me. "Look honey I know I was being a bit mean to you earlier" the sun had went down. I swatted at my arms the mosquitos were trying to bite me. "I see you can hold it down yourself and that is what we need in this family." "Okay no hard feelings." We hugged. I went to find Rashad I was ready to go there were too many bugs out now. The moon looked beautiful that night as we rode to his house. I put my fingers in his hands and it felt so right. Why had I not met him years ago? Why did I have to go through all that pain? I was sitting there wondering. I did not love Rashad, but I knew that I could get there with him. I loved to be near him so far and I think that if I could put up with Bruce and Hakeem, I knew that getting along with Rashad would be no problem. I was an easy going, lady who could deal with any situation as long as he showed me love then I could love back. "What you think about me making you my fiancé?" He asked. We had never discussed it. When we got in the party that is what he introduced me as his fiancé. "I think that is great" I smiled. "But how am I your fiancé and hell we haven't even dated?" That was the truth hell Bruce and I relationship had just ended. "Look I don't need to go on dates and go through that bullshit to know that you are my wife. I knew it the first day we met. I just needed you to realize that. I needed you to handle that situation with Bruce. You know I could have just beat Bruce's ass to make him give you your companies. I wanted to see how you would handle the situation." He cleared his throat." Hell, I wanted to see if you was a weak bitch who would let him walk over you or if you was a bad bitch that would not take that shit. I need a strong woman by my side." I was happy that I had passed his test. Rashad was not only fine, but something was telling me that there was more to this man than I knew. More than Bruce knew. All the things that I found out about Bruce was a shocker. I was proud of myself that I had not let Bruce win. I was proud that although I had gone through so much that I had not let that make me a weak woman. All my life they had tried to tear me down, but I had overcome every time. "What about my kids?" I asked. I know he wanted me, but he had not even met Deena and Malcolm. "You mean our kids I am serious about this shit. I am thirty-four years old I need a woman by my side for all the shit that I go through. Can you be her?" I was about to answer him when he cut me off. "Now before you say yes then look past my good looks. Look past my money and think can you really be my wife? Can you wake up to me every day? Shit can you leave your home and come live with me? Can you be submissive and understand that I can handle shit?" He was serious and I wanted to cry. I had never had anyone ask me if I could handle them. But a woman is a man's gift. I guess I should have always been the person making the demands. I hope Rashad was serious and really did know my worth. I smiled instead of crying. "When's the wedding?" Rashad didn't say anything. He kissed my hand and smiled as we pulled up to his house. As soon as we got in the house, I was all over him. I made him lie in the bed and I worked that stripper pole. We were not going to be getting married if he could not please me in the bed. I shook my ass up against the pole. As I twirled my hips, I raised my dress over my head and took it off. I damn near fell but I held my own. I was a bit self-conscious about my stretch marks, but Rashad didn't seem to mind. I had on some boy shorts underneath my dress, so I turned around and started twerking. I had those cheeks going left and right. I knew he had seen all this before maybe better being the owner of a strip club. I was not giving up I was going to give it my all. "Girl bring your ass over here" he said I stopped dancing and turned towards him. I climbed on the bed and crawled to him. He had taken off his shirt, but he still had on his shorts. I kissed him and my pussy exploded in juices and I knew my panties were soaked. He grabbed the back of my head and brought me closer. His aggressiveness was turning me on even more. He smacked my ass and he moaned. He liked what he had. I tried to take control, but he did it first. He maneuvered and got on top of me. He grabbed my titties and started licking the right one in a circular motion. All I could do was moan as I thought about how much I wanted more. I reached for his shorts and undid them while he started easing down to my stomach. He kissed my stomach. He got to my pussy and stuck his tongue out. He licked the outside of my box and teased me. As he opened the lips of my vagina, I knew he could see it gushing. He kissed my clit and then he tongued kissed it. It felt so good. He had done it to me before but not like this we were comfortable with no one around. "Fuck that give me that dick," I moaned. He laughed. "Are you ready?" He kissed my clitoris. "Yessss" I moaned he was playing I needed that dick inside me right now. He still was eating it but somehow, he changed positions. Before I knew it, he was on top and he was putting his dick in me. It was big and I was not ready. "Damn" I said as his big dick squeezed in my tiny opening. "Calm down baby I don't want to hurt you." Rashad kissed my lips. He slowly eased into me and my pussy was pouring down. I did not know if it felt that good or if our chemistry was just that strong. He started doing a circular motion and I was getting to like the feel of it. At first it was hurting but as he worked his way in, I loosened up. I lift my leg up more so that he could deeper. "You like that don't you baby?" He deeply stroked me. "Oooh yes I do" I moaned it was feeling too good and I did not want him to stop. We made love that night for two hours. That night I think I fell in love. When we finished, we fell asleep instantly. When we woke up the next morning, he was still holding me. I moved his arms and got in the shower. I threw on one of his shirt and put on some boy shorts. I went downstairs and made my man some breakfast. I made waffles, bacon, I saw that he had some fruits, so I threw together a fruit salad. I made cheese eggs, hash browns, and oatmeal. I made a breakfast fit for a king my king. He must have smelled the food cooking because he came downstairs. "You hooking it up lil mama?" "Yeah" I said kissing Rashad's soft lips. "Go get cleaned up and come eat." By the time I got done cooking he was out of the shower and dressed. We sat and talked about the move that I needed to make. "We need to find us a house out here. Shit Deena and Malcolm need their own room. Our room plus an office shit maybe a guest room. Like four bedrooms should be okay." Rashad said stuffing his mouth. "What about your son?" I asked he had not said much about his son I wanted to know more. "Naw we ain't got to worry about that." He said eating his waffle. "My baby's mama disappeared with my son years ago. I don't know where she went or why? We were on good terms we weren't together. They might be dead." "They not dead. If they are you still need to know." I looked at Rashad to try and get a response, but he wasn't saying anything. "What you think about a dog?" I asked to change the subject. "Hell nah." We both had to laugh. We spent the rest of the morning together. I had to catch my flight back home that after noon. Tomorrow was the big day. Bruce did not know what I had in store for him. He thought that he was going to be rich I had news for him. I had my pistol though just in case he was going to act stupid. Tre said that he would sleep on the couch to make sure I was safe after everything went down. I appreciated him. He was like the big brother I never had. I was happy that Mya had found him for the both of us because he was a big help to all my problems. He had done so much, and he did not even ask for payment. I could tell he really liked Mya because he was helping me. I was her lost, always having problems friend. Sometimes I wondered what they really thought of me. They always helped me, so I guess it was not a big deal. I was just ready to get this entire ordeal over.

Chapter Twenty-One
ANIYA

M onday was the big day! Mya came over and we did our paperwork as usual. As we ate our McDonalds breakfast we waited for the call. At about twenty minute before ten the phone rang. The manager I had hired to supervise at my home building business was there and Bruce showed up. I put him on speaker. Ken was a big guy and he was also Tre's big brother. He was a felon who was out of work and since Tre had been such a big help to me, I was willing to help him. He was laughing hard when I picked up the phone "Ken what happened stop laughing?" I started giggling because he was laughing. "Man, so we out here getting this work done and Bruce pull up. I had already let the fellas know what was going on when I came. They was cool, we getting this work done. Of course, Bruce walks up to me. He like who are you? I tell him like Ken I am the new boss you looking for work?" I burst out laughing Ken was a funny guy. He knew who Bruce was he just wanted to piss him off. "He looks at me real cocky and was like work I own this here company so how the fuck is you the boss? I tell him like well Ms. Turner hired me. He looks at me crazy and then he goes off like that bitch must be out her mind still trying to run shit like she the owner. Look man she misled you he tells me. This is my company and she has no say so, so you fired. I take out the copy of the paper and give it to him." He clears his throat. "What happened after that?" I smiled. "He got pale you would have thought he was a damn ghost. He stormed out of here mad. I don't know Ms. Turner, but you need to be careful because I think he may be coming to your house." I looked at Mya she looked scared. I wasn't I had my pistol. Let him come knocking at my door I was going to put two in his head without any remorse. Chance had been helping me with my kickboxing. When I told him about this situation, he advised me to get a gun. He had opened up his martial arts studio with the money I had given. He was a big help.

I was happy that when I did get a gun, he took me to the range. He told me how to clean it and put the bullets in. The first time I held that gun I thought I would be scared but I did not feel fear all I felt was power. I was good at kickboxing and after a week at the gun range, I had the perfect shot. I was not tripping off of Bruce. "Thanks Ken honey I know how to take care of myself. You make sure they stay in line at that place okay." I think that Ken was a bit sweet on me, but I was not interested. When I had hired him before I went on my trip to see Rashad, I could tell he was feeling me. "Aight." He said and we hung up. As soon as we hung up Mya said what I knew she had been thinking. "You think he coming here?" She looked scared. "Girl I want his ass to come here and start some shit." I said and I meant that. I would put a bullet in his ass real quick. Good thing Mya would be here to back up my story. It was about lunch time when we got the call from Sampson. I knew that Bruce would head over to Sampson's office after he found out what we had done. Sampson called me breathing but out of breath. "He is in jail." He said sounding a bit afraid. I knew that Sampson was not scared but there is no telling how Bruce came into his office. "What happened?" Mya asked. "He came in here throwing shit talking about I tricked him and then security rushed in here. I am going to press charges." He said. That was good that was one point to my plan to destroy Bruce. See I wanted to destroy him exactly how he had tried to destroy me. "That is good. I am sorry for all of this Sampson you have been a great help though." I was happy that Sampson had held his own. "I don't like his ass anyway." He said we laughed and hung up. I was happy that part of my plan was working. I was hoping they would be keeping Bruce at least until tonight. I wanted Bruce to understand that I was not to be fucked with. He wanted t to screw me over when I was trying to put money in his pocket. From day one I was willing to work with him and all he was trying to do was screw me over. I had a pussy, but I was not about to be fucked. After years of abuse my mind had matured and I was not that same scared, unsure, Aniya I had become a woman who was strong and in charge. I went and got my kids from the summer camp they were in and I was happy that they were okay. For some reason I was afraid that somehow Bruce had gotten to them, but he didn't. Tre had called and told us that Bruce would probably be in jail for the next two days once he went to court. I called Rashad and he was looking for us a place to live. We had decided that the kids and I would move to Atlanta with him. Mya would stay and run my companies. I trusted her. "Hey baby what you been up to?" He quizzed. "Nothing getting everything done here so that the kids and I can come to you" I said hoping he still felt the same way. I did not know this was new to me you know dealing with someone who had no intentions of harming me. "Good shit I will have a house by the end of this week. I been seeing some nice shit but they kind of pricey. I got about $75,000 I can put on the house, but I really don't want to be in too much debt." Rashad did not know that I was a millionaire. I had not told him any of that I wanted him to like me because of my personality. "Well you know I am going to sale my house so baby I can put some money on it too." "Hell, naw baby you just sit and relax I got this." I respected him for doing this for me. "You got the kids baby you just make sure y'all are straight." I agreed with him only because I wanted to see what he could do on his own. A real man will make a way and that is what I wanted to see from him. I knew the way that I wanted to live, and I knew that he would need my help. For right now I would sit back and see him work his magic. "Baby how we going to pay for the wedding stuff?" He got quiet when I asked him that. "Damn I got to think because shit I am trying to go to Vegas for the honeymoon. I will figure it out. Don't you worry." He said. I was happy that he was being a man. We talked a bit more and then hung up. The only thing I was taking was the kid's bedroom sets. All the stuff in their room but I was selling the house with the rest of the stuff in there. I had some of my employees clean out the house and paint. We had not heard anything from Bruce or about Bruce. We knew he was still in jail thanks to Tre's connection. He couldn't even make the $5,000 bail. I found a buyer to buy my house and I really gave them a deal I did not care about the money I just wanted to move on. Rashad was having a problem with the houses. I told him that I would come and help him because I was ready to leave. He agreed although he wanted to do it on his own. His income was not enough to get the house he wanted. Plus, I thought it would be a good idea for him to meet the kids. It had been several days, and Bruce had been released from jail. I had booked the kids and my flight and finished packing the little things we had left. I was getting my Porsche shipped along with the kid's furniture and our clothes. I had a few things in a suitcase, but I packed everything else. I was ready to make a change. I had been answering the kid's questions all day and I was tired of it. I had to handle one little thing before we left and then we would be on our way making a brand-new start. Malcolm wanted to know who was this man Rashad? How long had I known him? What happened to Bruce? Why did we have to move? The boy wanted to know too much. Deena of course really did not know what was going on. She did ask me a very important question and it brought tears to my eyes. As we watched television, she asked "is he going to be our new daddy?" I looked at her and my heartfelt heavy. Those type of questions made me sometimes regret what I had done. I put her in my lap, "no one can ever replace your father. We not looking for a replacement okay honey. Rashad will be your stepfather that means he will be helping Mommy because Daddy had to go to heaven." I really hoped she understood. Mya came later that evening to take us to the airport. I was happy to go, and Rashad was happy that I was coming. I hugged my best friend as we got ready to board our flight. "Mya you guys better come visit us." Tears fell from my eyes. "Of course, honey I love you Niya and I am so happy that you are my friend." She said and that brought tears to my eyes. I had never trusted anyone as much as I trusted Mya, she was my ride or die. I gave her a hug and the tears just kept falling. I had finally found someone who I could really trust. Now I was leaving her. I had someone here with me all this time and I was putting my trust in all the wrong people how foolish of me. I had to control myself. "I love you too. I am so happy that I finally let you in to my life." I said laughing. She laughed too. "I know right shit you a tough cookie to crack. And my babies!" She hugged Deena and Malcolm. I could tell it was hurting her to part from them. "Listen if anything happens to me you come get my babies okay Mya." I was serious she was the only person I trusted to get my kids. "Don't talk like that you about to get married and live happily ever after." I was happy she said that. I needed someone to be positive because although I was happy, I was still worried. We parted ways and we got on the plane at first Deena was scared but Malcolm loved it. He was such a big boy and I was happy to have him. He held his sister hand the entire time and kept her calm. We touched down and I was happy to see my man Rashad. He was standing there when we made it inside the airport. I introduced the kids to him, and you could tell that they were shocked to see another man besides Bruce. I had told them, but it was still new to them. They were especially surprised when Rashad got on one knee in the airport and purposed to all three of us. I was laughing and the people were standing around watching. I said yes. Deena said yes and I knew he had won her over. Malcolm however, was not impressed. "I don't know you," Malcolm said.

Rashad laughed. "I like you little man that's right you don't know me. You gone get to know me we gone kick it." I knew he was going to win Malcolm's little heart over too.

BRUCE

Monday shit hit the fan! I could not believe these black monkeys had tricked me. I go to the work sites to check on shit and some big ass, black nigga is there. I tell him his big ass better get the fuck out of here! He shows me papers saying that I am not the owner of the companies that Aniya was. I damn near lost my balance. I had to look at the papers again. After that shit I ran to my car. I looked at my papers and low and behold he was right! I had signed in the wrong spots! ANIYA the BITCH and that black ass monkey SAMPSON! I sat in my car looking in the mirror this shit could not be happening. My white skin turned pale and I was sweating. I needed to see Sampson. I started up my ca r and drove wildly to his office. I didn't knock or anything I stormed right into his office. As soon as I pulled out the papers, he was stammering talking about it was nothing he could do. I picked up the computer screen off his desk and it missed him by an inch. I was pissed and I was seeing red. Sampson was going to die but security came and took me away. They put me in jail, and I was pissed. The only person I could think to call was Teresa. She bailed me out and she made it very clear that she did not want to see me anymore. As we drove to my house, I noticed that Teresa had a ring on her finger. My blood was boiling as I looked at her. I composed my anger as she parked in front of my house. It just couldn't be over with us. Teresa put the car in park and turned to me, "I am serious Bruce. This time I am serious. I am in love I don't want you anymore it was fun while it lasted." All I could see was black as I put my hands around Teresa's throat. This bitch didn't want me then she wasn't going to love anybody else. All the shit that I had just been through a nd she said that it was fun while it lasted, she had me fucked up. She clawed at my hands and I squeezed harder. I released her neck and her lifeless body slumped over to the side. I looked at myself in the mirror and I was dripping in sweat. I jumped out of the car and ran to the driver's side of the car. There was no one outside as I carried Teresa's deceased body into my house. The weight of her body was heavy across my right shoulder. I struggled as I unlocked the door. When I made it into my house I was in disbelief. I threw Teresa's body to the floor. There was a big banner that read I AM A FUCKING SLUM, A FUCKING RAPIST! I ran to the banner and ripped it down. I looked at my walls and there was writing in lipstick it read I SHOULD KILL YOURSELF NO ONE LOVES ME! I ran to the bathroom and went to get a towel there was no way this was happening. Once I got to the bathroom the mirror read SISTER FUCKER! I could not believe this was happening I wet the towel and tried to wash the words away. The images came back to my head so vividly. The things I had done to Rebecca and her friend. I had gotten help I was not that person anymore. I ran to the living room where I discovered Teresa's body on the floor. What had I done? I ran to her and grabbed her face. "Teresa! Teresa! I am sorry baby!" I cried. This could not be happening. I was better off dead. I slowly walked to my bedroom and grabbed my sleeping pills. I just needed to get some sleep this was not happening. I had spent most of my time up while in jail so I just needed to get some rest, and this would be all over. I put a pill in my mouth and grabbed a bottle of soda to swallow the pill down. The soda tasted a bit odd, but it was going to help me get to sleep. I drank some more of the soda and laid down in the bed. Everything would be okay, everything would be better once I woke up.

Chapter Twenty-Two
ANIYA

I got the call about four o'clock that morning and it was like a dream. It was Mya she was frantic. Rashad and I were snuggled up in the bed together I slept like a baby when I was next to that man. I don't know if it was the sudden ringing of the phone that had frightened me or what, but I jumped out of my sleep. "Hello." "Girl it's Bruce" I knew what she was going to say before she said it. "He's dead" she said frantically. "What?" I said acting surprised "how? What happened?" I said sounding worried. I had woken Rashad up by this time. "I don't know but Tre said one his co-workers were talking about it and he put two and two together." She said. "Damn that's messed up. Look I got to go and tell Rashad what happened.

Are you okay?" I asked. "Yeah I am alright it is just scary." I didn't have anything to say and the silence was uncomfortable. Finally, we hung up and I looked at Rashad. "Bruce is dead," I told him. He laid back down "so our plan worked good shit let's get some rest fuck him." I agreed and I was happy our planned had worked. Rashad had told me about the woman Teresa and about how Bruce probably was using me to give the money to her. I was hurt broken, but I picked myself up. Duane was Darien's pen buddy. They had set it up where Teresa thought that Duane was loaded. She had picked Duane over Bruce that was number one. Number two he didn't have any money. I knew Teresa would come to Bruce's rescue and that he would get mad when he discovered that Duane had proposed. I figured either Bruce would get mad and want to kill Teresa or he would get mad and actually kill her. She was an unfortunate causality in this game. Once he saw all the shit, I wrote on his walls then he would get upset. Usually when Bruce was upset, he took a sleeping pill or some type of pill. He kept a refrigerator full of Coca-Cola next to his bed. I had spiked all of the bottles with Antimony. If not those bottles, then the bottles in the kitchen would surely kill him. No one was going to ask for an autopsy. No one was going to care that Bruce was dead they would be happy that he was gone. The cops would assume that he killed himself after he killed Teresa, that was the plan. After Bruce was sleep, I had my backup plan. Duane came into the house in the middle of the night and blew his brains out to make it look as if Bruce killed himself. There was a small and I mean tiny part of me that felt like Bruce did have some type of feelings for me. He had to I mean I am not a bad person he just didn't love himself so he could never love someone else right. Rashad and Malcolm had been gone all day. I asked Rashad was he going to Bruce's funeral and he said "hell no." His father had called and told him the news and he had pretended to be shocked as well. Deena and I were chilling in the swimming pool when they came back that evening. Malcolm came running to the back. "Mama! Deena! We found the perfect house." He said he had me scared for a minute. Rashad came around the house about a minute later. "Calm down boy. Let me talk to you for a minute baby." He said to me. I made Deena get out of the pool and go upstairs and change it was dinner time since our men was home. We went upstairs into our room so that I could change also. "Baby we did find a house it is perfect, but it is a lot of money." He said. "I don't think I can get it on my income. I told Malcolm that I would tell you about it but to not get his hopes up. He is excited." "We can go check it out in the morning" I said kissing him. "Okay but it is a lot but man it's perfect." He smiled. I wanted to see this house that had my men smiling so hard. When we pulled up to the house it looked like a castle. It was huge. Deena was jumping up and down in the backseat and Malcolm had a big smile on his face and so did Rashad. "You see it Mommy." Malcolm squealed. I nodded my head. It was a house fit for royalty and we were royalty I was the queen, Rashad was the king, and we had our prince and princess. I wanted to see the inside. We couldn't see the inside of the house, but we peered through the windows. It was a bit dusty, but I knew with the right renovations it could be the house of my dreams. "I want it!" I said to Rashad. "I do too baby but it's too much. It's over a million dollars." He said. I knew that this house would be pricey, but I wanted it. I had good credit and I had money in the bank I know they would give us a loan to cover this. I had over a million dollars in the bank. We still had to plan our wedding and I definitely wanted it to be a day to remember. Plus, the honeymoon and we had to furnish the house. Yes, I definitely needed a loan. "We will go to the bank in the morning." I said. That night I dreamed that I was drowning. As I tried to fight through the water, I saw Hakeem and he couldn't breathe. Then I saw Bruce and he had a gunshot wound to his head. I knew I was feeling guilty. They both had done me wrong. Yes, I could have just left the both of them but something inside of me wanted to see them suffer. What if there was some evil inside of me that I could not control? What if Rashad was an evil guy? What if he was going to harm me and my kids? My mind was swimming in thoughts before I knew it, I was screaming, and it was just not in my dreams. Rashad shook me up out of my sleep. "Baby what's wrong?" I was sweating and I needed to tell him. I had kept it a secret for so long and it was taking its toll on me. I had not told anyone what I had done the only one who knew was Chance, God, and me. I don't know why but I was ready to tell Rashad hell I had just murdered his brother with his help so I think I could trust him. "I killed him I killed my baby's daddy." I said. There I had finally told someone it was killing me inside. "What? What you talking about?" He asked looking confused. I broke down and started crying. I did not know why I wanted to tell him, but I did. I told him everything about how Hakeem had beaten me. I told him about how I had met Chance and he had taught me to defend myself. I let him know that it was my idea to kill Hakeem. I thought he was going to start beating my kids well

Malcolm in particular. I let all the shit off my chest, and it felt good. "I was not always this coldhearted I swear baby I was not this coldhearted." I said in between tears. Surprisingly he just held me in his arms. He held me tight and it made me feel like it was the right thing to do by telling him. I knew he was not going to judge me because he had helped me with the plan to have Bruce kill himself. "Calm down you not coldhearted you did what you had to do baby. I ain't gone judge you I am just happy you told me. At least I know I have a rider on my side and if push came to shove you will be willing to kill a person. The cops wouldn't even know it. You smart you kill and leave with no trace." I had never thought about it that way. I was killing without it being traced back to me. I had killed Hakeem and caused him to die from natural causes. I had devised a plan to make it seem as if Bruce had killed him. No loose ends I had no ties to my past. When I wanted someone gone I did just that. Was this something that was embedded in my DNA that made me think like a killer? Most people would just leave. Most people would have called the police on Hakeem and filed reports. But not me I decided that he needed to die, and I did not want to be blamed for it. I could have let Bruce have the companies. I could have tricked him and went on with my life, but I wanted to make sure he was not living. I wanted to make sure he did not keep coming after me. I really had no reason to want him dead because truthfully I had won. Rashad held me that night, but I did not sleep. I thought about everything I had gone through. I knew that I was not coldhearted, but I could kill if I needed to. I stopped worrying about things and closed my eyes. Bruce and Hakeem deserved what they had coming to them. I was the victim and I had survived.

Chapter Twenty-Three
ANIYA

The bank let us get a loan after they ran my credit and saw my bank account. Rashad looked a bit pissed when we left the bank and I did not understand. "What's wrong with you?" I asked. I thought that he would be excited about us getting the house. Here he was acting mad about what I did not know. I had on my brown, green, and pink sundress. It was a humid day in July, and I was not feeling this heat plus his attitude. "Why the fuck you ain't tell me you had all that money in the bank?" He slammed the door. I could tell he was making the kids nervous. They had witnessed their father and I fighting so much. I was hoping that he was not planning on hitting me because I was not trying to fight. "What you mean? You never asked I told you we could get the house. Why the hell you so mad?" I was tensing up this time and I was hoping he was not a woman beater. Damn I sure knew how to pick them. "Cause girl you had me worried and shit about all this stuff and I didn't have a reason to." He turned and smiled. "Girl you got that bank! Shit you should have told me I got plans for us." "What you mean?" "Stick with me and I am going to take us places." He started the car. "Damn two point five million dollars damn!" He was happy I turned and looked at the kids and they were smiling too. "Let's go talk this realtor down so we can move in our castle." He laughed he was excited! It made me laugh and I got excited. I had a family. I had a family with Hakeem, but I wasn't happy. Rashad made me happy and I hope it would stay this way. I didn't want to have to kill him too. "I love you Rashad." I said and I meant it. He looked at me and smiled. "Damn about time" he said. "I loved you as soon as I saw you. I knew I wanted to make you my wife. I love you too." That made my heart flutter. I had finally found someone that really loved me. He accepted my kids it was time to get our dream house. The day that we moved in was the day of Bruce's funeral. Rashad did not attend. His mother came to the house later that night after we got done. She was looking a bit tired.

She had not gone to the funeral. "This is a beautiful house." I led her into the family room. The kids were in there watching television. "These your kids?" I nodded my head, "I will go get Rashad." I had to walk up two flights of stairs. Our room was on the left side of the house. We had a six-bedroom house with four bathrooms. Four of the bedrooms were upstairs. There were two on the left side that is where our room was with a master bathroom. We was using the other room as an office. The other two was on the right side and that was where Deena and Malcolm was going to have their rooms. The other two rooms was downstairs in the basement of the house where there was a bathroom. The other bathroom was by Malcolm's and Deena's room. The other two bathrooms were downstairs on the first floor. One was in the back of the house and the other one was in the front of the house. I walked up to the door and I could hear Rashad talking on the phone. "Yeah man we moved in finally." There was silence so the other person must have been talking. "Naw I ain't told her." He was silent again. "I am going to tell her damn man. She perfect too, man." That is when I interrupted. I wanted to know what I was perfect for. I hope Rashad was not playing with my emotions. "What am I perfect for?" I asked. I was sort of mad and I did not want to show my anger. Rashad was shocked and turned around. "Call me back bro," he said and hung up the phone. I started walking toward him and he stayed seated on the bed. "What am I perfect for?" I asked again. He grabbed me and put me on his lap. "You perfect for me." He said and kissed me. Nope I was not falling for the bullshit. "For real what was you talking about?" Rashad eased me off of his lap. "I will tell you once Moms gets here." He said and started towards the door. "She already here." I said and became nervous. I hope my kids were okay being left alone with her. "Okay well come on." I told him to give me a minute. I waited for him to leave and I went and grabbed my pistol. I was going to be prepared. I made my way downstairs. I could hear them talking in the family room with the kids so that was a good sign my kids were okay. I went downstairs and they were in there watching Malcolm and Deena was dancing and singing for them. Rashad said, "look at my baby girl she gone be a singer." He said and that just made Deena hit her notes a bit higher and louder. She was off key, but he was gassing her up. "Look baby they gone be some stars." He grabbed my arm. "Okay kids can y'all go in the other room we gotta talk." Rashad said. The kids listened to him and I sat down next to Rashad and his mother sat across from us. "Since you are marrying into the family it is time that you know." His mother started and I looked at Rashad. I thought to myself what had I gotten myself into. "We are a family a very special family. We are looking for individuals to complete our family." I did not get what she was trying to say. "My son Darien is in jail trying to get connections so that we can become an empire again." "I don't get what you are trying to say." "My father was once the biggest drug lord across the nation." Rashad said "he was going from state to state supplying people that is how he met Bruce's mother. Up until Bruce raped and beat Rebecca our father was doing well. Bruce caused my father's mental breakdown. His best friend Cliff was supposed to run things for him while he got our family together. His friend disappeared with the money to keep the business running. We are close to finding him and we are close to building our empire only this time I will be running things." I listened intently this was a lot to swallow. "That is why I bought that strip club from Al Richards he is the connect and I need to get in good with him" I really did not know what to say. Hell, I had been forced to be in a relationship for almost a year. I got beaten on by a man that rescued me. Hell, all this man was doing was trying to build a drug empire. Who was I to judge I had killed before and I would do it again if I had too. Now I knew why he said I was perfect. "So that is why you said I was perfect. You know that I killed before and that my mind is corrupt." "Yes," he said and grabbed my hand. "I knew it was something special about you. Not only that but you are a hustler, you smart, beautiful I loved the way you ate up Mr. Richards at that meeting. Bruce was trying to play you and you did not lie down and take it. You devised a flawless plan and carried through with it. Bruce although he was my brother, he wasn't shit a waste of air. Now we can breathe deeper because he is gone. We can suck up his air now." He laughed. His mother laughed and I laughed. That was true he was a waste of air. Renee, Rashad's mother left after dinner and I got the kids ready for bed. I went to get in the bed I was tired. I went and laid in the bed with Rashad. He asked me what I thought about what he had told me. We had not talked about it since they had told me. I had not thought much about it neither, it was the last thing on my mind. Everybody was a bit flawed look at me I had killed my baby daddy and my boyfriend. Hell, I was not exactly picture perfect. "Well you can think about it if you have too." He said. I looked at him and gave him a kiss. I looked into those beautiful eyes and I saw myself. I saw what I wanted. Hell, I had taken a leap of faith with everyone else why not with this guy? I had two beautiful kids and he accepted them. I had so much baggage and so did he. We were willing to compromise. "All I am trying to think about is what colors we wearing to our wedding." I said and he gave me a kiss. He was happy and I was happy. Two weeks later… It was the day of our wedding and I must admit I was nervous as hell. Mya and Tre had flown to attend the wedding. Mya was my maid of honor. I was at the shop with her and we were getting our hair done. Mya decided on an updo for her long curly hair. I got a black long sew in something plain and simple. "Girl I am so happy for you." She said as we were getting finished. "Girl I am happy for myself all the shit I been through." I said. Mya looked at me. She placed her hand over the scar on my lip. "I know." "Remember if anything ever happens to me come get Malcolm and Deena." Although I was getting married, I still wanted to know that I had backup. "Girl shut up you gone be okay." She said, "now go marry the man of your dreams." I married Rashad Anthony Thompson the man of my dreams in the backyard of our dream house with our family and friends with my beautiful prince and princess to witness it was perfect! Everything was perfect until I had to kill Rashad.

To Be Continued…

ABOUT
THE AUTHOR

New York Times & International Best Selling Author
Billie Dureyea Shell was born in Compton California and
now lives in Ladera Heights with his wife and
kids who he loves to spend time with.
He is the Owner of several properties in the Los Angeles
area and gives back to his community by providing low
income housing to those who need it.
He stated "It doesn't matter where you at or where you
from it's what you do with your time. There's nothing you
can't do if you put your mind to it".